PERFECT LITTLE FLAWS

JENNIFER ANN SHORE

Print ISBN: 978-1-7360672-5-3

For Kilroy,
whose eyes burn
like wild prairie fires

ONE

It's not polite to eavesdrop.

I've lost count of how many times my mother has scolded me with some variation of that sentence, but whatever the number, it's clearly not enough, given that I continue to do it.

Usually, I hover just a little bit too long outside my father's study while the two of them argue about money, work, me, or whatever else, but I've also been known to crane my neck *just so* to pick up whatever conversation is happening a table or two over at a restaurant.

I've seen my mother's sneer more than any other expression on her face lately, which usually forces me to feign sheepishness without actually planning on breaking the habit.

It's not like I'm committing a moral or ethical violation when I listen to what's happening around me. In fact, I firmly believe I should be praised for my skills of observation, not damned for them.

And if people don't want to be overheard, why discuss things so openly and in public? Why should I, a mere seventeen-year-old, be the responsible one in every situation? Especially now, when two of my classmates are choosing to talk—very loudly, by the way—about the latest gossip in my town.

A little reluctantly, I do see my mother's point at this moment.

Because it's not like I'm technically *hiding* in the bushes, but I am completely obscured from their view, giving them the illusion of total privacy.

I remind myself that even if I were in their field of vision, they would probably carry on in precisely the same manner because they likely have no idea who I am.

Our school is massive, collecting students from all around the city and shoving them into a three-floor monstrosity, and I only recognize the pair because one of them has hair in a very distinguishable shade of pink that definitely blurred by me in the hallway last spring.

Greene High feels like a prison most days, which is why I'm here in my favorite park, documenting the last days of summer with my camera. Soon enough, I'll be enclosed in walls with windows so small they might as well not even exist.

I'm content to sit here, surrounded by greenery and flowers, with pieces of mulch digging into my elbows, snapping photos and taking in the park-goers' mindless drivel until I hear a name that startles me out of my creative process.

"Vince Novak." The blonde sighs happily, and the air that expels from her lungs as she utters those words makes it seem like the weight of that name is a relief to vocalize.

I lower my camera to see the pink-haired girl gazing at her friend with bored curiosity.

"Isn't he a soccer player?"

The smirk fixes itself on my face before I even realize it surfaces.

Because he's not just any old soccer player—he's *the* soccer player.

"Yeah," she answers, smacking her gum between her teeth. "He's supposed to play in the next Olympics and has, like, all sorts of scholarships lined up to go to these big schools. But he's had professional teams trying to sign him since he was, like, I don't know, twelve."

Her friend is not impressed by the list of accolades. "Okay?"

I don't admire those qualities about him, either—even though I once would have—but I understand those things mean something to some people.

Maybe it's just that I've heard the name Vince Novak so many times over the years that I'm numbed by it.

Or I wish I was.

"Well, he's transferring to Greene this year."

The gasp, thankfully, catches in my throat.

As much as I can hope this news is some sort of mistake or rumor based on wishful thinking, I have a difficult time believing that anyone would get off on spreading this misinformation.

I blink rapidly, thinking of the circus that will undoubtedly come with his arrival and realizing the best I can do is try to avoid it completely.

3

"So what? I don't care about some *soccer player*," she says like the term means less than nothing to her.

The other laughs, and it's one of those shrill sounds that somehow manages to drip with smugness. "Have you ever *seen* Vince Novak?"

I squeeze my eyelids shut, taking deep breaths as she pulls out her phone.

They *ooh* and *ah* over what seems to be every single photo on his social media feed, gushing over his eyebrows and cheekbones—of all things—then speculating about his relationship status. Apparently, a girl who consistently appeared in his photos last year is now nowhere to be found.

At first, their conversation piqued my interest, then it slowly tugged at my irritation, and now I'm simply wishing they'd shut up so I can concentrate.

I try to shake off their words by renewing my grip on my camera, pulling the viewfinder up to my eye and focusing on what's in front of me.

Most photographers want their photos to be perfect. Regardless of the subject, the goal seems to be capturing bliss in a single moment of time, as if every single moment in existence is flawless and framed correctly. Bonus points if it needs minimal editing before it hits their social feeds.

But I'm not most photographers.

In fact, most days it feels like I'm barely one at all, making more mistakes than actual print-worthy shots, but every single time my finger presses the shutter release, I learn something.

I like to find the little anomalies around us...the flaws

that get brushed by or ignored outright in favor of something more normal, more pleasing, more perfect.

And that's why I'm lying on my back, staring upward at these little sun-damaged petals. Despite the dryness of the summer, they've fought so hard to flourish, and I appreciate their valiant effort.

As a cloud rolls over, I snap a few photos in succession, loving the way the shadows cast an ominous haze on an otherwise cliché beautiful afternoon.

I groan when I see I'm out of space on my SD card, resigning that it's time for me to call it quits since I stupidly forgot my backup memory at home, then I stand and wipe the mixture of soil, dirt, and mulch off my legs.

"...and, yeah, he chose Greene even though every school in the district fought to have him transfer there for his senior year."

"So, he's really good, then?"

"Uh huh," the blonde girl says lightly. "They're calling him the next Jake Montgomery."

Her tone makes it seem like it's a salacious piece of gossip.

And maybe it is to everyone.

To everyone except me.

Her casual tone is like a stab in the gut—not the clean, neat precision line of a scalpel, either. It's a serrated knife wound, inflicting damage that's nearly impossible to repair, leaving the kind of complications that are tangible with even the slightest movement.

I guess this is what I get for eavesdropping.

If only I had less storage or more willpower, I could have avoided hearing this part of the discussion, but fate, or whatever has subjected me to this, is not on my side today.

I walk quickly back toward one of my favorite trails along the lake and try to appreciate the beauty of the area and the activity of the families who are enjoying the afternoon, but I can't.

All I can think about is Jake.

It's been more than two years since my brother died. I've had no other option but to make peace with it, but there are little unexpected moments, like this one, where I'm tossed into the deep end of the pool of memories in my mind.

It's taken me a long time to figure out how not to drown in the recollections and the sadness, but some days it's more difficult than others.

Really, it's Vince Novak's fault.

I've been aware of the comparisons of their playing styles for years, but his decision to switch schools and put on a Falcons uniform is going to make everything so much worse for me.

While I have yet to see Vince play in person—and never plan to—I can recall nearly every goal my brother scored and the celebration dance that went along with them.

Jake was a whirlwind on and off the field, and everyone loved him for his effortless charm, kindness, and cool head.

In my life, most of the stuff that has happened, is happening, and will happen is because of my brother… which sounds melodramatic, but it's true. My childhood revolved around his insane schedule of practices, games, and tournaments, but I was more than happy to play second fiddle.

I didn't fall into the trope of being the beloved baby of the family because Jake was everyone's favorite, shining so bright there was no choice but to be wholly mesmerized by his light.

Even in his absence, I still feel him with me.

Most of all when I pick up the camera.

Jake used to get obsessed with new things—baking, fencing, painting, whatever—in the brief breaks between soccer seasons and training.

He told me once that he used the time as an experiment to see if he could possibly love anything more than the sport.

It never happened.

But out of everything he tried, the camera was the only thing that stuck around, collecting dust on his dresser long enough to interest me.

The first time I held it in my hands, it was due to a fleeting moment of boredom, but I've barely put it down since.

Now, I'm so deep in the nostalgia spiral that I don't trust myself to hold it in my hands any longer, so I delicately place the camera in my bag and pick up the pace away from my classmates. I can't believe Vince Novak is going to be one of them soon enough.

This boy I've never met, who has been compared to my brother for years, will be attending Greene.

My school.

And Jake's.

If I'm being honest with myself, it feels like the school is really just Jake's, given that there's an entire shrine of his achievements by the athletic office. I have to take the long way around to most of my classes so I don't see the pictures of my dead brother every damn day.

As I reach the edge of the park, I try my best to shake off my thoughts, crossing the busy street that separates the park from a little ice cream shop.

It's basically a glorified wooden shack that somehow offers up the best soft serve ice cream in Western Pennsylvania. Although I haven't fact-checked this information for myself, considering I have a best friend who has spent his entire summer giving me free cones, it wouldn't be right to question that statement or take my patronage elsewhere.

"Miss Maren Montgomery," Andy calls, leaning halfway out the little window at the counter to spread his arms out.

"Mister Anderson Crain," I retort, then fall easily into his massive wingspan of an embrace.

He pulls back to take in my expression. "Is it a twist day?"

I nod, smiling tightly. "With extra sprinkles, please."

"That bad?" Andy asks, professionally groomed brows arching up toward his hairline.

He gets too much enjoyment out of assigning flavors to my moods.

Even though I have an overwhelming *sense of feelings*, according to him, I'm defined just fine in the only three flavors available:

Vanilla for when I'm pensive.

Chocolate for when I'm angry.

Twist for when I'm in a tizzy of emotions that I'm trying my hardest to get out of.

Then there are the add-ons for when I need a little something extra—sprinkles or chocolate dip. I've only gotten the latter once, and it was so messy and I complained about it so much that Andy took it off the list of my available options.

Today, he swirls the cone under the machine until it's perfect, then adds a generous portion of rainbow sprinkles before handing it over to me.

"Thank you," I say, eagerly accepting it from him.

"So, you going to share what's on your mind?" he asks.

I shrug and sink my teeth in, marring the pristine surface.

Andy scrunches his nose at me. "I've known you my entire life and have happily fed you ice cream during every shift this summer," he says, taking off his hat to run his hands through his long, brown hair. "And I'm still disgusted by, yet also slightly jealous of, how you impale ice cream with your two front teeth."

"One of my very few talents," I admit with a smile before biting into a particularly sprinkle-heavy area.

He rolls his eyes. "That and evading my questions."

I wipe my mouth with the back of my hand, giving myself a second before I have to start this conversation with him. "You know Vince Novak?"

"Vince Novak?" He pauses as if deep in thought. "Is that last year's district-leading goal scorer? Who's already being scouted for the Olympic soccer team and MLS? And is basically soccer's second coming?"

I balk at him, finding his words suspiciously similar to the conversation I overheard just a few minutes ago.

"I was bored earlier," he admits, sliding today's newspaper across the counter.

There's one of those old-school metal stands across the

9

parking lot that *The Pittsburgh Review* still fills every morning, even though I'm pretty sure Andy is the only one who deposits a quarter—that he may or may not steal from the register—to get a copy.

I tilt my head to get a better look.

Sure enough, at the top of the front page, there's a callout with news to flip to the sports section for the latest updates on the hometown soccer star.

I do so and scan the article, which offers an overview of his very impressive stats and performances before diving a little more into his decision to transfer schools for his senior year.

Vince credits the sudden change to the caliber of the coaching staff and his desire to win a high school state championship before he graduates.

I'm a little too familiar with the blind arrogance that insists winning is the only thing that matters, so I slide the paper back toward Andy, needing to get it out of my sight.

"Too much?" he asks.

I swallow and nod, then force my attention to the little drips of chocolate and vanilla swirl that have made their way down my fingers.

"Well, I'm having a great day, thank you for asking," Andy says, toning up his bitchiness, which is a very welcome distraction from my inner thoughts.

"Oh yeah?"

He flicks the corner of his name tag. "Look at this."

He puffs out his chest, giving me a better look at an assortment of rainbow stickers and the "HE/THEY" he scratched under his name, signaling his pronouns.

I smile, partly because of his excitement but mostly

because, no matter the situation, he's his most genuine self.

"And how is your bigoted idiot of a boss going to feel about this?" I ask.

"The owner won't love it. But Michael, his son and my shift manager, is secretly a fellow member of the alphabet mafia, which I discovered last night..." He trails off with a telltale smirk on his face.

"You didn't," I say with a laugh.

"Oh, I *so* did."

I chew through another half-melted bite, mentally picturing Michael's gangliness. "Isn't he a little young for you?"

"He's in our grade," Andy says defensively. "And I'm pretty sure he was in Trig with us last year."

"You haven't asked?"

"We haven't done a lot of talking."

"*Anderson!*" I scold without managing to suppress a smile.

"Oh, stop. It's not that kind of silence, and even if it was, who cares? It's mostly been a lot of *staring*, like they do in all those regency romances you made me watch last winter. It's pretty thrilling, honestly."

I listen actively as I slurp down my ice cream, and once I finally make it to the crispy cone, I bite it off in massive chunks until I'm so full that I have to throw the rest away.

"I think we're going out, like, officially tomorrow night," Andy continues, then lets out a loud exhale. "He finally asked me out in the walk-in freezer. One last hurrah before school starts, and I'm one step closer to being done with this place."

He taps his long fingers on the counter, showing his impatience with being stuck in high school for another year.

Andy doesn't exactly have a plan for what he wants to do with his life, but he knows that it's as far away from here as possible.

I can't blame him for wanting to have a fresh start somewhere else, even if it means leaving each other for a little while. I'll be sad to be apart from him, but I consider myself grateful to have had him as a best friend for all these years.

It all started when we sat next to each other at recess, slightly unsure how to spend the time.

When I told him about how Jake helped me climb on top of the monkey bars at the park near my house, he suggested we try it out for ourselves. Our teacher wasn't exactly enthused by our behavior and eventually made us stop, afraid we'd fall off the top and break our necks.

Even though we've far outgrown that phase of our lives, we've stuck by each other no matter the situation—dealing with conservative and overbearing parents (him), forgotten homework assignments (me), and bad experiences with dating (him).

I reached a whole new level of gratitude for him when my brother died. Facing Jake's death without Andy sitting beside me would have been even more unbearable because somehow his chattering on and on about nothing in particular was the comfort I needed to face the worst days of my grief.

"Why are you looking at me like that?" he asks, snapping his fingers in front of my face.

He'd probably be delighted for me to open up about *my feelings*, of all things, but he doesn't take compliments well, even if it's one of complete appreciation and offered with enthusiastic reassurance that he's absolutely going to do anything or be anyone he wants far, far away from here.

"I love you, you know that?" I say quietly.

He snorts. "Maybe today was a vanilla day after all."

I pick at my chipped nail polish. "Maybe."

"You know, if it's that easy for Vince Novak to switch schools, who says we can't?" Andy demands vehemently, pulling his hat back in place as a car pulls into the parking lot. "Try again with new, secret identities somewhere else."

"What kind of secret identity are you trying to take on?" I ask.

"I don't know, but it definitely includes some sort of French accent."

I quirk an eyebrow. "There's more than one French accent for you to pick from?"

"I can't believe my best friend is such uncultured swine," he breathes.

I laugh. "It's probably time for me to take my very sheltered, American self home."

He waves me off and plasters a big, fake smile on his face to welcome the new customers while sliding the tip jar to a more prominent position on the counter.

On the drive home, I crank the windows down and turn up the music, extending my arm outward to catch the warm air in my palm. The motion, combined with the sugar, somehow calms me down.

At least, until I step through the front door.

It takes me all of five seconds of eavesdropping to know

13

I'm walking into chaos. I don't even have the energy to listen to what my parents are fighting about, but given my own emotions and discoveries today, I have one guess as to what has upset them.

Vince Novak.

He's coming for my brother's district records, and if the projections are correct, he's going to annihilate them.

The fact that their son is going to be dethroned from that legacy is enough to handle, but the fact that the usurper is going to do it in a Greene Falcons uniform, with the same coaching staff and on the very same field as Jake…

I get it.

I don't agree with it.

But I understand it.

I kick off my shoes quickly and make a beeline straight to my room, briefly touching Jake's door as I pass, like I've done thousands of times before, while hoping that things aren't going to be as bad as I think they will be.

TWO

The first day of school is overwhelming, even under normal circumstances.

Our school is a maze of long hallways and doors that you think are classrooms but are random storage and heating closets.

I try to take comfort in the fact that even though I have to pull out my schedule to double-check my next destination every time the bell rings, it'll eventually become second nature like it does every year.

But somehow, the information seems to fall out of my brain as soon as I tear my eyes away from it.

With so many students, there's no shortage of opportunities to make new friends and test out different personalities, haircuts, and clothing styles—usually without too many lasting social repercussions—but the nervous energy everyone feels on the first day always compounds into making me fall into a heap on the couch at home.

This year is different, though, leaving me to feel even more stressed and emotionally charged.

And it's all because of Vince Novak.

No one cares that Judy Cooper buzzed her hair or that Adam Williams grew seven inches over the course of the summer because Vince is all anyone can talk about.

If I wasn't already exhausted by the mere sound of his name over these past few weeks, I would likely have more patience for the buzz around his attendance, but it's only lunch, and the day has already felt twelve hours long.

Andy and I wedge ourselves in at the end of a table with a massive tray of cheese fries, ignoring the invisible dividing line between us and a group of friends who pretend we aren't there.

"Where's Michael?" I ask him.

"Haven't seen him since our date."

"Well, if you're *dating*, doesn't that include eating lunch together?"

He shrugs. "Maybe it does, maybe it doesn't."

"What does that even mean?"

"It means—" Andy suddenly stops, glancing just above my head toward the entrance of the cafeteria. "Oh no."

My gaze snaps over that way, as I'm worried something awful has happened, but I merely get to witness Vince enter through the double doors.

He's surrounded by what can best be described as a mob.

Students of every grade and social group seem eager to push closer to him, calling for his gaze, and the rest of the attention on him is from the hundreds of others already seated, who gawk at him.

I'm full of shame about being included in that categorization.

It's not his obvious attractiveness that gets me, although it's hard *not* to notice it, but the look of absolute disdain on his face.

The severity of his features is heightened as he crosses the cafeteria, looking dead ahead as he moves with confidence that's absolutely impossible to ignore.

I take in the hard line of his square jaw and his dark, determined eyes, and I'm surprised that it's such a drastic change from the indifferent yet slightly smiling face in his headshot that usually accompanies articles about him.

"I take that back," Andy mutters. "I should have said, 'Oh, yes.'"

I briefly turn back to my best friend, who is making a big show of plucking up a soggy fry—saving the crispy ones for me—and dropping it in his mouth.

If only I could be as carefree about this situation as my best friend is…

Instead, my irritation for Vince Novak is like a bomb waiting to detonate. It has festered, building up inside me over years of hearing his name, the fights my parents have had about him, and now his presence here. I contain it as best I can, burying it deep in my chest cavity while also waiting for the day it explodes, leveling everything in sight.

If Vince didn't want this attention, he shouldn't have made such a big, public deal about switching schools—and if he really expects to be some big star, dealing with a few overeager students is the least of his problems.

Besides, he should consider himself lucky; it's probably

every transfer student's dream to have a line of people waiting to eat lunch with them.

Not mine, though.

I, myself, sneak off to the art room whenever Andy's absent.

But now, I try to ignore whatever is swirling in my mind, as I take in the way people fawn over Vince. It's not just girls, looking to score with him—although there are plenty of those—but also a number of guys wanting to befriend him, and oh, goodness, at least one teacher who approaches his table.

Vince seems to tolerate his teammates among the crowd well enough, but it appears as though everyone else is beneath his attention.

Eventually, when yet another person talks at him, he grows bored enough to let his gaze wander around the room.

Most people boldly stare back at him when their gazes meet, but when his eyes catch mine, I'm so flustered and embarrassed at being caught that I turn around in time to see my best friend blow him a kiss.

"Andy," I hiss. "Stop that."

He balks. "Just trying to be a friendly face."

I roll my eyes, standing up before the bell rings and leaving him with the french fry mountain. "I'm going to art now."

"Fine," he sighs. "Just leave me here with a week's worth of calories and an unobstructed view."

Unlike me, Andy has no problem forcing himself into conversation with the others at the table once I leave him, which oddly comforts me as I take the long way to class.

I feel lighter with each step closer I come to the safe haven that is Owen Wilde's room. It's my favorite place in the entire school—maybe even in my small world—and it's been three long months since I've seen it.

When I enter, and breathe in the slightly toxic air, I realize it's the closest I've ever felt to coming home, like I can truly feel comfortable. The sensation is aided by how the space is overcrowded with easels, endless tubes of paint, and various other materials, with dried splotches dotting every surface.

It's a messy contrast compared to the clean, sleek lines of the lens and body of my digital camera.

This is partly why, even though I love photography, I don't think of it as an art, necessarily. But I'm grateful Mr. Wilde disagrees with me and lets me use the period to hone my skills.

As other students file in, I perch on one of the stools off to the side by the window. It's my favorite spot because it overlooks a miniscule, overgrown courtyard while also giving me a full view of the room.

I see a few familiar faces, along with a handful of new ones who are looking at the various paintings, sculptures, and materials with wide eyes.

"It's organized chaos," Mr. Wilde says by way of welcoming the students once the bell rings. "And it's art."

To an untrained eye, it looks like a disaster in here, but I know how carefully curated this mess is because I've spent more time here than in any other place in this school.

Sometimes I wish I could move into this room instead of living in the same house as my parents.

"My goal this year isn't to get you to adapt to traditional

JENNIFER ANN SHORE

techniques or even to color within the lines—"

He earns a few chuckles with that.

"—but to get you to find your own inner talent, explore it, and make it tangible."

I swear, from anyone else that line would be ridiculously cheesy, but out of his mouth, it's like poetry, leaving us all hanging on every syllable.

"That said, I do have to adhere to state-mandated curriculum requirements, and therefore, I must give you this," he says, holding up a one-page syllabus.

He walks around the classroom, distributing the sheet and greeting every individual person, but when he gets to me, his demeanor changes, like he sees me as a loyal friend instead of a student.

Mr. Wilde—Owen, when it's just the two of us—has a secret smile that's just for me. I've seen it so many times that I'm usually desensitized by it, but after a summer apart, it nearly stops my heart.

Andy teases me about having a crush on my teacher, but honestly, although I have two working eyeballs, it's so much more than that. I respect the hell out of him.

He's been all over the world—visited museums, explored new cities, and worked diligently to improve his own art before he eventually settled down here a few years ago to collect a steady paycheck and establish roots.

"If you'll look at the first paragraph..." Mr. Wilde starts.

We spend the rest of the period reviewing the syllabus, then students ask him questions about the different pieces around the room.

He has a charming story for everything, and the students eat it all up like it's candy.

It's no surprise, really, that he manages to become everyone's favorite teacher.

Well, *almost* everyone's.

Andy no longer has the patience to listen to me gush over him, but part of me thinks it's because he's a little salty. When he took art sophomore year, he spent the time socializing and messaging senior boys on the football team, so he barely ended up passing.

I don't feel *that* bad for him, really.

The room is pretty deflated when the bell rings, which occurs too quickly for my liking, but we're all off to rinse and repeat the syllabus-and-intro process for the next period.

"Bye, Maren," Mr. Wilde calls as I exit.

I'm one of many students leaving, but I'm so elated that he specifically called out to me that I can't help but turn and offer him a small smile before I rush to my next class.

Unfortunately, my history classroom is all the way on the other side of the school. It wouldn't be so bad if I didn't have to take a longer route to avoid the athletic department hallway and the pictures of Jake.

After I walked by it the first time, I went home and begged my parents to have the school board remove the overlarge reminder of his passing, but they refused, saying it was nice the school wanted to honor Jake's memory.

Easy for them to say since they don't have to see it on a recurring basis.

But I think they like the idea of someone outside the three of us thinking about him regularly, as if it somehow keeps him alive.

It also has the added bonus of absolving them of their

guilt for locking away every picture, trophy, and memory associated with him in his bedroom.

As the bell rings, I *just* make it across the threshold of my history class.

My former self—the one buried deep inside my soul—is laughing at how out of breath I am.

Jake would certainly be embarrassed at having such a sedentary sister.

And this is the problem.

Not my level of fitness but the unexpected little reminders of him that seem more like a plague than a privilege—particularly at this exact moment as I wind my way to an open seat in the back of the classroom.

My inner thoughts are validated further as I nearly choke on the scent that brings me back to happier days.

Citrus.

The familiarity of the light, fruity scent convinces me that I'm smelling a ghost—not of my brother, necessarily, but of the past—until I nearly fall into my seat.

I breathe through my mouth, trying to avoid picking up any lingering orange notes, and see the source of it all.

Vince Novak.

Because *of course* it's him in front of me, with only an empty desk as a barrier between us.

As I process this, my brain also registers subtle hints of clove and cinnamon, like he's a personification of my favorite season.

He's facing forward, completely unaware that I'm having heart palpitations because of him.

And for as much as I've been forced to think about him these past weeks, I think it's pretty unfair.

I pretend to listen to my teacher drone on while I glare at the back of Vince's head.

When Jake and I were kids, my mom would cut up oranges as a halftime snack for his Saturday morning soccer games, and before they got packed away in the cooler, we would steal a few little wedges and put them in our mouths, making it look like we had orange teeth. We thought it was the funniest thing in the entire universe. Our mother, however, was unamused.

Even after his games grew more intense and he didn't require a mid-game treat cut up and provided by the parents, he still kept up the vitamin C intake, claiming orange juice was the best recovery drink.

He was such an evangelist for the practice that even our grandma down in Florida heard about it and mailed us two boxes of oranges every winter.

I think about Jake every single time I see or smell an orange—which, now that I think about it, isn't that often. It's not a staple in our cafeteria, and most guys prefer to drown themselves in artificial woodsy scents that usually give me a headache.

If anything, this trademark scent gives me more reason to steer clear of Vince Novak at all costs, and I mentally add it to the growing list.

The teacher ends her spiel a little early, so we're all left with a brief reprieve to socialize before our next class. Most heads turn to Vince, seeing if he'll say or do anything interesting, but after a full two minutes of him keeping his eyes cast downward, the blonde girl I recognize from the park moves her chair closer to him.

"Hey, Vince," she says coolly. "I'm Julia."

He turns, but even in profile I can see his reluctance to engage with her. Obviously, I can't read him completely, but he does offer her a curt and somewhat dismissive nod.

She offers him a warm smile, not reading the signals or simply ignoring them completely. "So, you play soccer?" she prompts.

I have to press my lips together to stop my laugh from escaping.

Even in my nonexistent dating experience, I'm not sure how this approach is going to be a success.

Still, for some reason, I can't help but watch the scene play out.

"Or do you prefer the term 'football' to be used?" Julia clarifies with a wide smile.

"Soccer's fine," Vince says, his voice barely loud enough for me to hear the words.

She nods, thrilled that he's engaging with her. "Funny, though, because it's a game played with your feet and a ball, and the sport we call 'football' is probably more fitting to be named 'soccer,' but I couldn't even imagine how that change would take place, even if calling it 'football' doesn't make sense. Which reminds me, it's so weird that our school is named Greene, but neither of our uniform colors are green! Like, who made these decisions?"

"Y-yeah," he says, blinking at her rambling.

He slowly turns his attention back to the syllabus in front of him, but I'm not sure that's going to save him from her persistence.

I can't help my smirk, but whether it's at her failed attempt at conversation or his exasperation, I'm not entirely sure.

THREE

It takes a few weeks for me to finally hit my stride, which is far longer than normal.

I've purposely given myself a course load that fulfills just the basic requirements for graduation, not needing to deal with the stress of honors or AP courses.

The career I want doesn't require a deep knowledge of American history or the ability to write at college level or wield a scalpel without squirming.

If I challenged myself academically, maybe I'd be more distracted from my home life, but instead, I've decided it would be better just to throw my entire mind into my extracurriculars, which keep me going.

Art club and working for the student-run newspaper are somewhat flexible, but both give me a little direction while still offering ample leeway to shoot what I want.

In the past, I've primarily used a digital camera, as it gives me an instant view of what I've captured and options for automatic adjustments of things like ISO and white balance. But last spring, Owen told me that he thinks it's important to continue "challenging the mind's eye."

Whatever that means.

It coincided nicely with some reorganization the art club worked on in the storage loft, and I came across a camera that looked straight out of the 1970s, with the bulky metal exterior, outdated design, and, most interestingly, no screen.

And so began my measured interest in film photography.

Over the summer, I studied as much as I could. I watched hours of videos on the subject to understand how to adjust from using a digital camera to developing film on my own.

Film photography is a dying art. The few places I've found around here that develop photos charge a ridiculous price, so that, combined with the romantic notion of owning my images from start to finish, means I wanted to learn to do it on my own.

Now, I'm getting the chance to put it into practice.

After the last bell, I happily make my way back to the art room and drop my bag on the table, breathing in the paint fumes and charcoal dust—canceling out the scent of citrus.

"Maren," Owen says, rubbing his hands together in excitement and causing the collection of silver rings on his fingers to jangle.

I smile at the sound and let my eyes wander up his forearm, from his tattoos—all of which have their own fascinating stories behind them—to the way only he can pull off a faded logo shirt, unbuttoned vest, and skull cap.

"Owen," I return, finally meeting his eyes. "Are we ready?"

He nods. "Let's do it."

I follow him back out into the hallway, and we don't stop until we're standing in front of a faded oak door.

With my hand on the knob, I feel a little bit like a character in *The Lion, the Witch and the Wardrobe*—my favorite movie as a kid—about to venture into Narnia.

I take a breath, then open it, only to be met with a thick, dark curtain.

"There's a slight gap in the door frame," Owen explains, pulling it aside and ushering me forward. "This should keep everything out, though."

I glance around the space, finding it pretty comfortable, given that it once housed nothing but art supplies and unstrung canvas materials.

There's enough room for the two of us to take a few steps between the "dry side" of the workspace, containing a wooden desk and storage area for the proper materials, and the "wet side," where a makeshift sink sits, along with the trays that will hold the chemicals we need to process and develop the film.

"The most difficult part was the ventilation," Owen points to the silver cover on the ceiling. "The janitor owed me a favor, though, and we got creative."

He turns off the main, yellowish-tinted light and flips another switch, casting a reddish hue over us and everything else in the room.

"It's perfect," I gush. "I can't thank you enough."

I've already decided this is going to be my own personal refuge. My bedroom at home is private, but there's always a chance that one of my parents will barge in to lecture me or I'll be disturbed by their near-constant fighting, which is loud enough to hear over whatever is coming through my headphones.

I'm ridiculously grateful that Owen believes in my talent enough to want to nurture it—not only that, but he spent his summer days getting a space set up for me to use.

I can only hope to repay his kindness and support someday.

"There's something else I wanted to talk to you about," he says, flipping the light switch and stepping out of the room.

"Oh?" I ask, reluctantly watching him sigh and close the door.

We walk back toward the art room in uneasy silence, and when he sits heavily on top of one of the tables, I'm a little jarred by the shift in his demeanor.

Owen is an emotionally expressive guy, but it's usually passion he exudes, not dejection. This is something I've never witnessed from him before this moment.

"Are you okay?" I ask.

He nods, then grimaces, rubbing his palms over his thighs. "This isn't exactly great news, and I shouldn't be burdening you with it your senior year, but..."

My mind races with possible scenarios, and I have to stop myself from snapping at him to hurry up and spill whatever is on his mind. Even though we're close, he's still a teacher, and I respect that boundary.

He pinches the bridge of his nose, seemingly needing a brief moment to compose himself, then looks at me with sad eyes. "The school board is trying to cut the art department and club."

"What?" I gasp in surprise.

"We're set through the end of this semester at least, but *apparently*, the soccer team's request for new goalposts and an overhaul of the ticket booth, among other things, is more important than fostering creativity in the community and offering a first-class art program."

"They can't do that," I sputter.

Owen's jaw ticks in irritation. "They can if we don't raise enough at the fundraiser—and our goal has doubled since last year."

I gape at the revelation, opening and closing my mouth multiple times, but I'm speechless.

"We'll figure it all out," he says with a tone full of resolve.

I don't agree with his sudden positivity.

Every year, we put on a fall art show, displaying the first round of projects that have come out of classes and whatever the few students in the actual club have to contribute. All the proceeds go directly back to the art department, but we barely make enough money to pay for a fresh round of supplies.

My parents never even bother to show up.

They attended every single one of Jake's soccer games and tournaments, supporting him year-round in all climates, but they aren't interested in dedicating an hour on a weeknight to come see my work.

So it's extra gutting that this could potentially all be taken away.

For freaking goalposts.

"It'll be fine, Maren," Owen says. "I just wanted you to be aware of what could happen. But I didn't mean to keep you so late."

I check the clock hanging on the wall and notice I'm very late for the weekly *Greene Gazette* meeting—which means I'll likely get stuck with the assignments Mindy, the other photographer, doesn't want.

"It's okay," I tell him, pushing down my irritation at the news and my tardiness as I grab my backpack.

"But, Maren?" His voice calls me to a halt. "I'd appreciate it if you didn't mention this to anyone in class. I'd like to keep the focus on a general note that our fundraiser needs to be extra successful, maybe push more students to volunteer their work."

"Sure," I say with a nod, then dash down the hall.

Mrs. Smith, the advisor of the newspaper, teaches Trigonometry, so the room we use for our meeting is pretty much the exact opposite of the lovely, overcrowded art room.

I just don't get the same welcoming feeling from calculators, triangles, and logic as I do from random bits of clay and paper.

It's a very practical setup, though. There's a row of computers in the back, used primarily by the paper's small team of reporters and a wall of corkboard material to tack up proof copies before they're sent to print.

Ella, the editor-in-chief, gives me a quick smile as I slide in, not missing a beat as she runs through the list of open projects.

After Jake died, she was one of the few people at school to approach me and offer her condolences, and while I don't do well with pity, she's been nothing but genuine.

I've always admired her ability to somehow be sharp and driven without losing her softness and relatability, and I think it's going to lend well to her becoming a successful journalist someday.

"And since Mindy's got a full plate..." Ella turns to me. "Maren, how about you team up with Amber for the feature? We just need a few simple studio shots."

"Sure," I say evenly.

I don't like taking assignments like those, which Ella definitely knows. I understand she can't produce an entire newspaper by catering to staff preferences, but I'm not looking forward to it.

Most photographers love a studio setting—having full control over the lights and atmosphere fosters creativity in them.

But not me.

I prefer the unpredictable outdoors—or at least an indoor setup with some action...like the girls' volleyball game I covered last winter or the robotics competition I documented right before school let out last June.

But that's not what I'm getting right now.

I eye the somewhat empty corner that I've seen Mindy convert into a makeshift studio in the past.

If I clear a few desks out of the way, I'll be able to catch better lighting from the windows—especially if we take the pictures right around this time.

With a general plan in place, I listen as Ella runs through the rest of her list, waiting patiently and hoping to get an assignment that's more aligned with my area of interest. To my disappointment, she finishes her spiel shortly after.

A few students beeline for the computers, but I stay rooted to my spot, pulling out my camera to flip through some of the shots I took after school yesterday, but I don't love anything I'm seeing.

Sometimes, if I take a photo I'm exceptionally proud of and there's a little space in the paper, Ella will publish it in one of the interior pages as an art feature.

"Maren." Amber greets me with a tight smile that doesn't meet her eyes.

During freshman year, she and I were friendly enough to have a few sleepovers at each other's houses. I wouldn't say we were exactly close—because nothing compares to my friendship with Andy—but it was nice to hang out with her.

However, when our class schedules didn't line up the following year, every passing interaction seemed awkward and stilted, so when we both joined the newspaper staff last year, we made an unspoken agreement to avoid each other.

Plus, our inability to connect is aided by the fact that after one of our staff meetings last spring, I overheard her talking about my "subpar" skills, saying I shouldn't be getting published just because people feel bad that my brother died.

I may not be the gold standard for what it means to be a good person, but even I can't wrap my head around that level of cattiness. It's almost impressive, actually, how she can think my photos are garbage and still speak to me about working together.

If anything, I'm a little envious that she can disconnect from her opinion and move forward with what needs to be done, whereas I'm dragged down by every thought swirling in my mind.

"So, for this," she continues, flipping her hair over her shoulder, "we're going to be indoors, for sure. We can talk about different poses or setups or whatever you're thinking, but I guess the first thing we need to figure out is the day and time. Does Friday after school work for you?"

Another opportunity to stay away from home? Done.

"Sure," I say. "That's fine."

"Because that was one of the tentative days I got cleared," she charges on, talking a mile a minute. "I mean, you won't believe the hoops I had to go through to even get this approved with his coach and his schedule, since it cuts into his practice—"

"Who?" I ask, even though I have a feeling I already know the answer.

She flinches at my tone. "What?"

"Who are we shooting?" I clarify, speaking slowly, then clench my molars together.

A mixture of pity, annoyance, and elation crosses her features. "Vince Novak."

I chuckle to myself.

Of course it's him.

Amber's forehead creases. "Is that going to be an issue? Because I could ask Ella to rearrange Mindy's schedule—"

"I'll be fine," I say plainly.

"Okay. Well, then, let's go ahead and talk about what I'm envisioning."

Despite the fact that I'm screaming inside, I keep my

expression completely neutral, letting her make absolutely absurd suggestions while I count down the minutes until I can get the hell out of here to go bother Andy at work.

I need some ice cream therapy.

It's definitely a twist day.

FOUR

"I asked Michael out," Andy says casually as he walks with me after school the next day.

I shoot him a sideways glance. "I thought you guys were already going out. You've been on, like, at least five dates and given me details. Actually, way *too many* details, I should tell you."

Andy laughs. "That was just hanging out. Like, the pre-dating stuff. Now we're all official and exclusive."

The squeal of excitement I let out surprises us both.

"That's great," I say coolly, trying to play it off, even though I don't need to. "Anderson Crain with a *boyfriend*."

He rolls his eyes. "I wanted to go with 'partner,' actually, but Michael said it makes us sound like we're cowboys or something."

I shrug. "It does seem more serious, somehow, but I'll use whatever you want."

"Of course you will," he says confidently, though his smile is a little sheepish.

My best friend has been out practically since birth, never shying away from being his true self, but that hasn't been the norm for the people he's dated.

In fact, this is his first official relationship since he was publicly scorned by a closeted baseball player during sophomore year, and although outwardly he didn't let it show, it shook him.

I know him well enough to realize he's a little more cautious these days—it's a huge step that he's moving forward with this relationship at all.

Despite the heartache, he's willing to open himself up to the possibility of being crushed while holding out hope that it's worth it.

I don't think I could ever be so brave.

"I admire you, Andy," I tell him as we near the art room.

He rolls his eyes. "Who doesn't?"

To everyone else, that confidence is charming, but truly, it's a deflection of his real feelings and fears.

"I mean it," I urge, tugging on his arm to beg him to take me seriously. "Having your heart completely obliterated, then finding a way to patch it together and offer it up again takes a lot of courage."

"Courage, stupidity, desperation, who knows really?" Andy says flippantly.

I scoff. "Well, not to detract from your news…" I start, drumming my fingers on the doorknob.

"It's why I'm here," he reminds me. "Detract away."

I swallow, then open the glorified closet that's serving as my darkroom and chuckle at the unimpressed expression on his face.

"Well, this is it," I tell him, pulling the curtain aside.

He steps in, eyeing the space warily. "This is it," he repeats slowly.

"Oh, come on," I groan. "Stop being so judgmental. It may not be some state-of-the-art setup, but it's really nice for what I need. I mean, it's safe to use—"

"Well, that's reassuring."

I ignore his tone. "It's perfect, Andy, and I'm thrilled."

His nose crinkles. "You're telling me your *dreamy* art teacher *Owen* spent all summer on this, and this is the best he could do? It's a little creepy. I mean, a teacher setting up this very enclosed darkroom just for you and everything."

"I told you not to call him that," I snap, elbowing him in the ribs. "And if you're going to make fun of it, then get out and go to your shift."

Sensing he hit a nerve, Andy backtracks and spins slowly. "It's not the worst space ever, I guess, and if it helps you revive an outdated process, then go for it. Vintage is always in, so why not?"

"I am going for it," I say evenly.

"Well, then, don't let me keep you," he says, smiling sweetly. "I must go serve frozen milk and sugar to the masses."

He drops a kiss on the side of my head, emphasizing the *muah* sound, then leaves me to it.

I take a few breaths to center myself.

As much as I wanted to show off my new space to my best friend, I'm equally content to enjoy it solo and get lost in the silence and the process.

I take my time figuring out my bearings, gently double-checking that the chemicals and materials are in the same places I saw yesterday with Owen.

It's not a professional setup by any means, and frankly, I think a few corners were cut in regard to what's typically used.

But at the very least, even if I don't have the fancy viewfinders and brushes, I have the proper lighting, the three chemical solutions, and the paper that will make this possible.

After I left the newspaper meeting yesterday, I wandered around the park, taking pictures with varying colors and light and objects. They aren't my favorite shots by any means, but I wanted to capture different styles to see what would come out the best when I develop it myself.

Though I don't have high expectations for my first round.

The red bulb flickers on with a flip of the switch, and I close the door, then gingerly pull the curtain across it to ensure that cracks of the regular yellow-tinted fluorescent light from the hallway don't seep through. It's a precautionary measure because I read that even the briefest exposure to light can damage the process.

These materials aren't exactly cheap, and if we're worried about the art budget already...

I snap on a pair of rubber gloves, renewing my focus on the task at hand.

In theory, it's simple, but I'm a little nervous as I pop open the film canister and select my first negative, snipping it off from the others and lining it up to project onto the paper.

Once it's captured—through a quick-flashing light mechanism—I grip the paper with tongs and slide it from one solution to the next.

I'm absolutely giddy when the image starts to appear.

After rinsing the photo in a water bath, I carefully hang it to dry on a tacked-up line of string, keeping the clothespins as close as I can to the edge of the paper so it doesn't damage the photo itself.

From what I read, it should take about an hour to dry, so I use that time to develop more photos, getting more confident as I go.

There are a few splotches, and some of the edges are blurred, but if anything, the imperfections make me love the outcome even more.

The process of making my work come to life is so cathartic.

Just as I've hung my seventh attempt, there's a rush of noise in the hall, and before I can register what's happening, the door opens.

I screech, grateful that the curtain is doing its job and protecting my photos, but as the person responsible for the disturbance gets caught up in it, I slam the door closed, hoping nothing is ruined.

My nostrils pick up on that same orange, clove, and cinnamon scent from yesterday, and I dig my fingers into my palms, letting my anger out silently as the intruder untangles himself from the black material.

"Whoa," Vince says, stepping back from my glare. "Sorry, I'll just go."

"No," I say quickly. "Don't open it."

He blinks, then nods, and I turn, desperate to check my work.

"Did I mess them up?" His voice is calm and smooth, but I find it grating.

Part of me wants to say yes just to spite him, but the truth is, I don't actually know how to tell—that wasn't a part of my research.

Still, I take my time to try and figure it out, letting the red hue of the lighting set the tone of silence between us as I stare at the drying photos, and luckily, I don't see any discoloration or other damage.

"I think they're going to be fine as long as the light doesn't come in again," I say as much to him as myself.

But I need to test my theory.

I select my next shot, and as I work, I pay even closer attention to the development, looking for an indicator that the light had an impact.

Seeing none, I breathe a sigh of relief.

Vince clears his throat. "Is that...a dead bird?"

"Yep," I answer in a clipped tone.

It's my favorite of the pictures I took yesterday because even though it's a little morbid, it's also beautiful.

I don't normally find dead animals appealing, but there's something about the way its body is situated with its wings spread out, as if defying both death and gravity while taking its final flight toward the ground.

At the time, I thought it was poetry, but looking at it now, it's kind of...

I don't even know.

I reluctantly turn to face Vince full-on, attempting to discern his expression, but instead, I pick up on that easy confidence of an athlete, like he's never once questioned whether he belongs somewhere—even though he should be out on a soccer field, not in a converted closet.

In his simple shirt and joggers, I can still see how lean and strong he is, an impression that's rounded out by the stunningly sharp features on his face. Up close, his allure is even more overwhelming than the pictures, gossip, and glances across the cafeteria let on.

I blink, realizing I've been scrutinizing him for far too long, but he doesn't seem to be bothered by it.

"We got off on the wrong foot," he says, extending a hand. "I'm Vince."

I look at his large, calloused hand like it's a reincarnation of that dead bird I photographed.

"I know," I say before I turn back to pick up another negative.

He lets out a long, loud breath, surely not accustomed to speaking to any female who doesn't fawn over him. "I'm sorry for interrupting. It's just that there was a small mob of freshman girls following me down the hall—"

"How terrible for you," I mutter, gripping my tongs in irritation.

"Right," he says, startled by my sarcasm. "And, uh, yeah, I just wanted to hide. I didn't realize I'd be interrupting anything."

I press my lips shut because this is entirely his fault, and I don't want to offer any words that soothe him.

He shouldn't have come to this school.

Shouldn't be chasing my brother's records and legacy.

Shouldn't have inserted himself into this one little area of peace I hoped to establish for myself.

"And obviously, I don't want to ruin anything, so, uh, I guess I can wait until everything is dry?" Vince suggests a little awkwardly.

"That'll take at least an hour," I huff. "When I finish with the negatives, I'll hold the curtain so you can slip out."

"Okay," he says. "I'll just hang out over here and let you work."

I try to lose myself in the movements once again, but I'm incredibly conscious of the way he's watching my every move with his arms folded across his chest, like he's some art critic.

I wish I had some music or anything at all to distract me from his overpowering presence, but all I can do is focus on my own breathing and the chemicals that are bringing my work to life.

He steps closer as I rinse off the next photo. "This is pretty cool."

I don't know if he's talking about the picture or the process.

"I thought you were going to stay over there and let me work?" I deadpan.

He smiles, and even in the darkness, I see the flash of white teeth and the slightly crooked left canine that throws off the perfect row.

It's that perfect little flaw, the slight imperfection, that catches my attention.

My hands twitch at the idea of capturing it with my camera.

"Maybe I could help," he suggests, bringing my attention back to reality.

"No, thank you," I say immediately.

I don't care if he's somehow the most gifted film developer—or whatever the correct job title is—in the world.

It's not even him, specifically, but it's the idea of *anyone* touching my photos.

I would never hand my work over to another editor to adjust on Photoshop, where changes can easily be made, let alone trust this annoying stranger with the one shot I have at getting these right—even though they're technically my test batch.

"Fair," he admits with a low laugh. "I guess I wouldn't trust you to take a penalty kick for me."

I snort at that.

If he only knew.

"So, why are you doing it this way and not just having them printed?" Vince asks, shifting uncomfortably, like he can't stand to have a moment without movement or noise.

I debate ignoring him, but I think that would build into some bigger confrontation that I'm not interested in.

"Our annual art fundraiser is coming up. Although I usually shoot digitally, I know how popular film prints are, so I'm hoping to tempt more people to buy something."

He nods, considering my words. "That's a great idea. When is it?"

"The first week of October," I answer.

"Spirit week? What day?"

I sigh. "Thursday night."

"Maybe I'll swing by after practice."

"I'm not sure our little fundraiser is worth the attention of big soccer star Vince Novak," I sneer.

He narrows his eyes. "If it's a worthy cause, why not?"

I laugh hollowly. "Well, we're trying to raise money to make up the difference of the art department's budget, since new goalposts and a ticket booth are more important, so that's probably a no-go in your eyes."

"Ah, so that's why you don't like me," he says, like it's some silly little thing he's been trying to piece together this whole time.

I don't correct him.

"But I don't know anything about that," he continues through my silence. "I'll have to ask Coach Eric."

I grind my teeth at that name. "It's not the coach's decision. It's the school board's. And it's out of your hands."

"Well, it couldn't hurt—"

"I'm done," I say abruptly, even though there are a few negatives that I *could* process if I wanted to.

I walk over to the curtain, stretch it out to its maximum width, and wait for him to leave, and I hate that my hands shake slightly because of the frustration I feel.

He opens his mouth like he wants to say something, but ultimately, he slips out without another word.

Once the door closes, I let my head drop, feeling like the weight of everything in my mind is too heavy. Then I sit for hours alone in the closet, contemplating every single emotion, until my alarm goes off, signaling it's time to go home.

FIVE

I know I'm right.

Talking to someone on the actual soccer staff won't do anything to resolve budgeting issues or save the arts program, but ever since Vince mentioned "Coach Eric," I haven't been able to stop thinking about it.

My brother also referred to him by that moniker, which my parents found amusing, but I chose the more typical "Uncle Eric," since he's not only my father's brother but also my godfather.

He was a fixture of my childhood, a constant presence at our house, and just as invested in my brother's future dazzling career as my parents were.

In fact, my father seemed a little jealous that his brother could talk to Jake about deep tactics and create an even firmer connection over the sport.

Until Jake died, of course.

Then the relationship between us all shattered.

I thought we were bonded, sharing love like a real

family, but it has become clear that I was delusional, thinking anyone cared about me more than for my place at my brother's side.

Even now, as I look at the absurdly large picture of Jake that hangs outside the athletic department, it's hard to believe we were all once as happy as he looks in this static moment in time.

Staring at his big, infectious smile—the same one I used to have in my own arsenal of expressions—along with all the awards and plaques with his name on them in the trophy case is like my own form of early-morning immersion therapy.

"Maren?" Uncle Eric says in disbelief.

It's been so long since I've heard his scratchy voice… He's constantly hoarse from yelling as he paces up and down the sidelines of the field.

"Hi, Uncle Eric," I say with a little nervousness.

He moves like he's about to hug me, but then apparently thinking better of it, he fiddles with his keys.

I realize in this moment that the only person who has hugged me in years is Andy, and as much as I love him, the thought makes me frown.

"Come in," Uncle Eric offers, pushing the door open and reaching over to flip on the lights.

"I brought you this," I say as I hold out one of the two to-go cups of coffee in my hands.

I splurged and got us treats at the drive-thru Starbucks this morning, knowing he's pretty much useless before coffee in the mornings.

Or, at least, he used to be.

I don't feel like I know him anymore.

"Oh, thank you," he says, accepting it gratefully and confirming that his lifelong habits didn't disappear in the last few years.

He takes a long first sip, and I try to stand proud as he takes me in.

My appearance hasn't changed that much since Jake's funeral, but I might look a little less hollow and thin than I did back then.

I still have the same light brown hair, hitting just below my shoulders. It's long enough that it's not totally unmanageable, and I'm able to pull it up into a ponytail, even though it's been years since I've even considered doing an activity that would require my hair to be out of my face.

"It's nice to see you, Maren."

I nod because, honestly, I agree. "It's been a long time," I say quietly, shifting my weight between my feet.

His mouth twitches, and I'm not sure if it's because he's fighting against smiling or frowning.

"And, I don't know, I just wanted to..." I trail off. "It's just been a really long time."

We both chuckle at my awkwardness and repeated words, albeit a little uncomfortably, until my eyes land on the shelf behind his desk.

He knows what I'm seeing the moment I stiffen, but I can't stop myself from moving to get a better look.

The frame is a little dusty, but I'd recognize my own work anywhere.

It's one of the first shots I ever took. Jake's figure is silhouetted by the light of our back porch, making him indistinguishable to anyone who doesn't know it's him.

I sold it at the first art show fundraiser after he died, but I didn't know who purchased it.

"Are you still taking photos?" Uncle Eric asks.

"Yes. There's another event—"

"To raise money to make up for what the athletic department stole," he finishes.

I'm surprised by the bitterness of his tone, but I nod.

"I'm sorry, Maren," he says with genuine regret in his tone. "I didn't have anything to do with it. I promise. I would never try to take something away from you, especially this, and after you've lost so much."

My throat grows thick, and I try to swallow the emotion.

I thought the hardest part of stepping foot in this office would be seeing my brother's eyes staring back at me, permanently fixed in the same position in the hallway picture, but the fact that my uncle supported my work without me even knowing, and then his apparent siding with me on the funding issue…

Well, I certainly didn't think it would happen—not that I really had any expectations upon barging into the office of a man I haven't spoken to in years, even if he is family.

My phone buzzes, and I check the screen to see a reminder from Ella about the photo shoot after school.

As if I would forget.

I've been dreading it since the moment I got the details, but I'm desperate to escape this situation, so I use it to my advantage.

"I have to go," I whisper to my uncle.

He nods in understanding, and before he can move to

walk me out, I renew my grip on my bag and bolt, grateful when he doesn't follow me.

I curse myself for thinking this was a good idea, and seeing as I'm not the type of person to let things go easily, I spend the first half of the day in a fog.

My mind serves up grainy memories, like textured snapshots from my print photographs, of all the time Uncle Eric, Jake, and I spent together growing up, and as much as I try to push them away, they linger.

I leave Andy hanging at lunch, attempting to get myself back to normal by hiding out in my converted closet. From my vantage point, huddled on the floor and inhaling snacks from the vending machine, I have to admit that my photographs actually look pretty cool.

I only slightly snap out of my trance when the next bell rings, relying on the sugar and salt overload to keep me going through the remainder of my classes.

After school, I shove two pieces of gum in my mouth and stress chew as I work on the lighting setup in an attempt to turn Mrs. Smith's classroom into a suitable studio while Amber reviews the final list of questions she wants to ask Vince.

I've got the backdrop set at the optimal position based on the light coming in through the window and the handful of studio lights I've spaced around, but I won't know for sure until I can test everything on Vince himself when he arrives.

Usually, I'd ask the writer to stand in, but Amber's petite frame is hardly a suitable substitute for Vince's height and broad shoulders, so I try to wait patiently.

But the lull gives me time to dive back into the

onslaught of memories, and for some reason I'm fixating on the last Christmas that we had when Jake was still alive and—

Vince finally announces himself with a knock on the door frame.

And for the first time, I'm actually relieved to see him, knowing his presence will distract me.

"Hello," he says confidently, striding in with one hand in the pocket of his jeans.

Amber rushes over to him, eyeing the way his soccer jersey hugs his torso. "Vince, I'm Amber. Thank you again for agreeing to this story and shoot. It's going to mean so much to our readers to get an exclusive sit-down with our new senior."

She continues babbling, not noticing that he's not paying her much attention.

He's not even looking at her.

Because his dark, unrelenting stare has been fixed on me since the moment he stepped over the threshold.

I drop his gaze, busying myself with nothing as they sit down, but I still hang on their every word.

Amber makes a big show of using a voice recorder and asking if it's okay to use it, wanting to come across as a professional.

"It's fine," Vince says with an encouraging smile, giving her his complete attention.

"So, Vince," she begins. "I know you've answered this in other interviews, but I wanted to ask you myself...why the transfer to Greene?"

He rests his elbows on his desk, forcing his physical self to relax.

I notice the shift in his demeanor.

Amber doesn't, though, because she's too distracted with trying not to drool all over herself.

I feel a little guilty for my thoughts because the last thing the world needs is more women pitted against each other, but my mind is simply processing all the facts around me.

Plus, I'd be lying to myself if I didn't admit to carrying a chip on my shoulder for the harsh words I overheard her say about my passion and ability.

"I wanted to join the fantastic team here and be coached by the best to have the greatest shot at winning this year's state championship," he explains with a grin. "It's a little vain, I'll admit, to chase a trophy, but that's kind of what we do as athletes. We play to win. And I knew transferring to Greene was the right decision for me."

I skimmed a similar version of this story when his interview came out in *The Pittsburgh Review* before school started.

But now, even hearing it from his mouth, I don't buy it.

His previous school made it all the way to the semifinals last year, whereas Greene barely made it to the quarterfinals before our best forward was taken out.

While I didn't see the game myself, I heard everyone talking about the nasty collision he had with the other team's goalkeeper.

"That makes total sense," Amber says. "Why else are you playing if you're not trying to win?"

He nods, clearly grateful that she's not going to push the issue.

"So, have you thought about what you want to do after you graduate high school?"

I roll my eyes at that question because if he hasn't signed and announced his decision by now, he's certainly not going to do it in the middle of the season to some high school reporter who probably doesn't even know how many players take the field.

Vince catches my gaze before shifting back to Amber, and I'm left wondering if he picked up on my annoyance.

"I have thought about it," he admits with a laugh, not missing a beat. "More than anyone probably knows. But it's such a big decision, and I'm lucky to have many offers. When I am ready to announce, I'm sure you'll be one of the first to know."

Amber blushes at that.

This is definitely one of the few times in my life where eavesdropping is actually very appropriate, but it still feels odd. Not the fact that I'm a bystander to this conversation but that I'm learning about Vince from the guy himself, and I'm not the one asking the questions.

"But do you have any goals?" Amber presses. "Or hints?"

"I don't think I've kept it a secret that I would eventually love to play for the national team, maybe even bring home a gold medal at the next Olympics."

"But didn't we just have the Olympics?"

I snort, then realize how loud it was and attempt to cover it up with a fake cough.

"Those were—" He stops himself, eyeing the voice recorder, and mentally edits his response. "The *summer*

Olympics are when soccer is played. Although it would be fun to try and play in the snow."

She laughs and, to her credit, breezes right past the fumble. "Let me take a look at my list of questions here...already got that one. Oh, I'm curious about this one. Who is your favorite professional player?"

"Megan Rapinoe," he says with no hesitation.

I gape at him.

Most male players would say Messi or Ronaldo or one of the current players on the men's national team, but to go for my own personal favorite player...

That is a surprise.

I used to have posters of her, Abby Wambach, and Carli Lloyd tacked up on my walls, but after Jake died and I distanced myself from everything to do with the sport, I tore them down.

Even now, I can remember what it felt like to rip the paper into pieces while trying not to completely fall apart.

I bite down on my tongue, letting the physical pain mask the mental one, and refocus on the conversation, which has apparently progressed on nicely without me.

Vince very patiently answers Amber's increasingly asinine questions, while I start to feel irritated at having to listen to them.

I could be outside, alone, taking more pictures, then developing as many as I can before the janitor kicks me out for the night, but unfortunately, I'm stuck here, waiting for this sham of an interview to be over so I can snap some stupid posed photos and move on.

"So, you're the main goal scorer for Greene?" Amber

asks in a singsong voice. "Is that the same position you played at your last school?"

I can't stop the words from spilling out of my mouth. "'Goal scorer' is not a position. The correct term is 'forward' or 'center forward,' but in some formations, he's slotted as an 'attacking midfielder,' which, yes, does mean he scores a lot of goals."

Vince grins at me while Amber's eyes narrow.

"Thank you for clarifying that," she says a little too sweetly before shifting her gaze back to Vince.

"She's right," he confirms with a smirk.

She switches away from that topic completely. "Is there an advantage of going to college first rather than straight to a professional team? Are there rules that say you have to be a certain age or something?"

It's not a bad question, actually, given that some sports do have restrictions in place about age and eligibility, but that's not the case in U.S. soccer, and I'm absolutely sick of her questions.

Plus, Jake wanted the entire "college experience" before he went pro, and look where it got him.

Not alive anymore.

And with that thought, my dwindling patience has officially snapped, and I'm not in the mood to hear whatever well-rehearsed answer Vince has on the subject.

"Are you almost done?" I ask, pointedly looking at the clock on the wall, as if I have somewhere else to be.

Amber rolls her eyes. "Are you going to keep interrupting?"

"Maybe," I bite out.

"Maren," she seethes.

Vince's eyes lock on mine, and I don't think he realizes he does it, but he mouths my name like he's testing the feel of it on his tongue.

Amber exhales in annoyance.

"If you don't let us finish, I'm going to have no choice but to tell Mrs. Smith."

"And tell her what?" I counter. "That it's my fault you're totally unprepared for this interview and don't even know what the hell 'zone defense' means?"

She huffs. "God, it's the *Greene Gazette*, not *The New York Times*."

"I could use a break," Vince says, smoothing things over. "What if we take some pictures, and you can ask me anything you want between takes? Or after?"

"Sounds good," Amber agrees, eager to appease him.

I nod, refusing outright to show my appreciation, and gesture for him to come over.

"I need to test some lighting, if you don't mind standing on the mark," I point to the little X I marked in duct tape on the linoleum.

He steps over, eyeing the setup as I move one of the lighting rigs to accommodate his stature—I don't recall him being *this* tall in our exchange in the darkroom.

"No film today, then?" Vince asks quietly.

I frown and shake my head.

Objectively speaking, he'd be one hell of a model to test out some of my more artsy shots on, but I'm not about to say that, so I'll have to settle for Andy or whatever inanimate objects I stumble upon in the park.

"Can you close your eyes for a second?" I ask.

He obliges without hesitation, like he already trusts me,

even though I've known him for one second and made it clear that I'm not his biggest fan.

I turn off the overhead lights and flip on the temporary rigs. "Okay, it's going to take your eyes a minute to adjust, so don't rush to open them. I'm just going to do some test shots for shadows and levels, so don't worry about posing."

I pick up my digital camera and click a few random shots, ensuring that everything is flashing when I want it to, then double-check the screen, wishing I had a proper external monitor setup instead of having to zoom in.

"You ready?" I ask.

"Sure," he says. "Smiling or no smiling?"

"Smiling," Amber pipes up.

Vince looks to me to confirm.

"Smiling's fine," I say.

He nods and grins, looking comfortable enough.

I grip the camera in my hands, moving around to capture him at different angles.

But my eye is repeatedly drawn to that one little imperfect tooth on the top row.

It's the focal point of my mind, and I need to break that fixation.

The few photos I take aren't good enough to even be considered for publication—at least for as long as my name is attached to them.

"No more smiling," I declare in frustration at my own fascination.

That makes him laugh. "That bad, huh?"

I click a few shots, noting the way his genuine laugh differs from his forced smile, but eventually, it falls off completely, and I'm met with a stare that's somehow intense and bored at the same time.

After snapping him from different viewpoints, I flip through the shots, then I glance around, trying to see if it's a lighting change that needs to happen or a different photographer.

When my eyes land on the soccer ball that Amber had the forethought to bring, inspiration strikes.

"You down to try something?" I ask, tossing him the ball with one hand.

He catches it easily and nods.

I place my camera on the tripod and quickly change some of the settings so the exposure and focus don't change.

"There's a technique called sequence photography, which is kind of like a human version of stop motion, or a photo version of a timelapse," I explain in layman's terms. "I'm going to set the shutter to release at repeated inter-vals, and it's going to snap every fraction of a second, then stitch the images together to show the motion."

I stop, ensuring that he's keeping up.

"Sounds cool," he admits.

"Do you think you can curve the ball right here from that short of a distance?" I hold my hand about a foot above the tripod.

"Not even a challenge," he says confidently.

"Are you sure you don't want to take more poses?" Amber asks, likely hating my suggestion because it's not typical for feature photos. "Maybe a few headshots?"

"I'm sure," I say.

Vince places the ball up at the perfect angle on the floor, then backs up a few steps.

I'm glad I cleared out the additional space, or this wouldn't have worked.

"Ready?" he asks me.

I hope he's as good as everyone says and not about to send a speeding soccer ball right through the lens of my camera.

"Go," I say, pressing the button, then putting my hands in place to catch the ball.

It's almost beautiful how easy it is for him to pull off the kick as the lights flash, and after I safely grip the ball in both hands, I pounce, eager to see the result on the screen.

"Oh, damn," I breathe.

"What?" Amber asks as she and Vince both come around to look.

"That looks awesome," Vince gushes. "I love it."

"Oh, yes, me too!" Amber agrees.

I smile, unable to hold back my enthusiasm. "It'd look even more awesome with a bicycle kick, but I don't want you to risk injury."

"I've got some ideas," Vince says with a grin.

We spend the next hour getting better and better photos with a variety of trick shots, and I swear it's the most fun I've had in years.

SIX

It's a feat I never considered even the remotest of possibilities, but somehow, the photos of Vince take his popularity to another level.

Even worse, I'm caught up in the crossfire.

In the weeks that follow, random people approach me before class and in the hallways to ask for details of the shoot. They want to know whose idea it was to take those kinds of photos and what Vince was like in person. Some of my classmates even encourage me to release more photos in upcoming issues of the *Gazette*, saying they can't get enough.

I find it ridiculously overwhelming, but Andy, of course, obsesses over the newfound attention I'm getting.

He strikes up conversations with people any chance he gets, while I wonder if selling Vince's photos at the fundraiser might meet a significant amount of our goal.

But I can't bring myself to speak to Vince again, let alone ask him for a favor and profit from him. I allowed myself to enjoy the moment of testing my photography skills, and he was a willing participant.

That's it.

And I don't even spend *that much* time editing the photos or staring at the first few shots I took where I can see his crooked tooth.

Besides, I'm really busy with homework, other assignments Ella hands off to me, and getting ready for the fundraiser.

When I'm not encouraging freshmen and sophomores to enter their half-finished art pieces or developing my own film, I'm lugging my camera around town, trying to find something that I would absolutely love to contribute.

I have a few contenders, but I haven't found anything, really, that I absolutely love.

But I'm out of time—the fundraiser is tonight, and I just have to hope that people see things in my work and want to support the arts program enough to bother buying one.

"Is it just me, or is spirit week more nauseating than usual?" Michael asks, sitting down beside Andy at lunch.

Ever since they became an official item, Michael has been a more regular fixture at our end of the table.

I don't know him that well yet, but I can see how happy Andy is, even if he doesn't let it show, and that's more than enough for me.

"Thank you!" I give my best friend an exasperated glance. "That's what I've been saying."

"Who doesn't love to dress up on theme days?" Andy argues, even though he, in fact, does *not* love it and did *not* dress up once this week.

I shake my head. "You know, I thought you would be more on my side after they cut you from the cheer squad last year."

"We don't speak of such things," Andy reminds me, nostrils flaring.

"I didn't know that," Michael admits with a chuckle.

"He was depressed for weeks after," I tell him. "Wore all black and everything."

Andy rolls his eyes. "Maybe I was just feeling chic."

"They're idiots," Michael says, sliding his hand across the tabletop.

It's not exactly a secret that they're together, but they don't go around publicizing their relationship when they're within the school walls, which is something that Andy has ranted about to me via text message many times.

However, in a cute but also somewhat bold move, Michael slips his pinkie on top of Andy's in a silent promise of support.

Everything else continues around me as normal, our classmates chatting excitedly about the soccer game tomorrow, completely oblivious to the very small but huge gesture taking place in their midst.

My gaze stays laser-focused on their physical touch, and I swipe my phone from my purse, open the camera app, play with the limited tools of light and exposure, then start taking pictures of their subtle contact.

"What are you doing?" Michael asks.

"Don't move," I command, shifting to get a better angle.

"She's in the zone, Michael," Andy explains. "Single-minded until her creativity is fulfilled, trying to capture reality as she wants it to be understood through her own vision."

Michael nods. "That's actually pretty beautiful."

I'm a visual person, not a wordsmith like Andy is—in this one situation, apparently—but the best way I can describe it is like an overwhelming itch somewhere in my chest that urges me to forever mark a moment before it's lost.

When I'm finally satisfied, I flip through the photos on my phone and smile.

"This one," I decide, turning the phone to show it to them.

"Very cool," Michael says.

"Cool?" Andy balks, shifting into his most pretentious voice. "It's *art*, darling."

I spend the rest of lunch editing the photo on my phone, and thankfully, the rest of the day goes by pretty quickly—even if each chime of the bell kicks my nerves up a notch.

It doesn't help that, after school as we set up, Mr. Wilde makes a grand speech about the importance of the fundraiser. His tone is light and encouraging to the group, but his gaze is heavy toward me, silently reminding me how much pressure is on the success of the event.

Following that, we all work quickly but not very efficiently.

The freshman volunteers mix up a few pieces, placing them with incorrect placards, and I have to rehang all of my pictures because they're crooked in their frames.

Eventually, everything is set for the event—all the pieces are on display, and the pictures are on the wall and the table at the front entrance—so I head home to get ready.

Driving usually calms me, but I don't feel at ease as I roll through the familiar streets. Putting my private work on display makes me feel vulnerable enough as it is, but now I feel pressured to monetize it, and I can barely keep my hands from shaking as I grip the steering wheel.

Maybe I'm not a fit for the cutthroat world of photography after all.

I chuckle to myself because I know that's not true. I don't have a choice in the matter.

I need photography just like Jake needed soccer.

The house is empty when I get home, so I head directly upstairs and jump in the shower, attempting to wash away all my stress.

I'm grateful that my parents are out doing who knows what so I can get ready completely unbothered, without concern of getting into an argument about my priorities in life.

"How long have you been sitting here like this?" Andy asks in an amused tone as he steps into my room.

I didn't hear the front door open or the stairs creak under anyone's weight, so I flinch slightly at the sound of his voice.

I'm still in my bathrobe, but at least I've finished running a flat iron through my hair and putting on my makeup.

"I don't even know," I admit.

I check the time, seeing that we should have left five minutes ago, and dart toward my closet, flicking through the options with a frown.

Andy sighs. "No, none of these," he bats my hands away from my own clothes.

I take a step back, recognizing I've already lost this battle, and notice that he's a little more formal than usual. The occasion is not exactly a grand event, but we're encouraged to dress up a little bit.

Last year, I think Andy wore a nice pair of jeans and a button-down shirt, but now, he's in an actual three-piece suit.

"What is this?" I ask, gesturing to his torso.

He continues his scrutiny of my closet, but I can see he's trying to suppress a grin. "Michael's coming tonight. Our first school outing together and whatnot."

"Of course, you wouldn't get this fancy just for little old me," I tease.

"Well, if you're going to be taking photos, I wanted to look my best."

Mindy, the other *Gazette* photographer, is officially covering the event, but I'm bringing my film camera with me. I never know when inspiration will strike—and, frankly, part of me feels empty when I don't have a camera in my hand, like I'm missing an extension of myself.

"This one," Andy says definitively, pulling a dress out of the closet.

"It's too short," I protest.

"It is not! It's, like, an inch longer than what our restrictive-ass dress code requires."

"How do you know? You haven't even seen me wear it."

Without another word, he shrugs it off the hanger, hands the material over, and turns around so I can slide it on.

When I do, I glance at my reflection, and I'm not totally disappointed by what I see.

I got this dress for some Christmas party at my dad's company, which I never even ended up attending, so it's definitely more mature than I would have picked for a high school setting.

It's simple, black, and sleeveless, and it'll do.

Andy was right about it hitting me perfectly mid-thigh, but I don't acknowledge it out loud.

"Well, I'm not wearing heels so—"

My objection is cut off when Andy turns around and shoves my slip-on loafers into my hands.

"Good," I say, dropping them carelessly on the floor and stepping into them.

"I don't suppose I could talk you into a little red lipstick?" Andy suggests, earning a glare from me. "It's just, as much as I love your natural look of Chapstick and mascara, maybe we could go a little bold with color? Maybe some eyeliner? And if you'd ever let me practice contouring—"

"Anderson," I snap. "Focus."

He nods resolutely. "Right."

As I swap purses, a devilish smile crosses his face that I absolutely do not trust.

"What?" I ask.

"Just thinking about Vince Novak."

I quirk a brow at him. "What about him?"

"Think he's coming tonight?" Andy asks innocently.

I scoff. "Why would he?"

"Didn't he say he'd try to stop by after practice?"

"He was probably just being polite," I argue. "Besides, that was weeks ago."

Andy lets out a big, dramatic sigh. "And what about the way he's been staring at you ever since you locked him in that closet with you?"

"I didn't lock him—" I stop, processing the rest of his sentence. "What do you mean staring at me?"

"Well, I don't think he's looking at *me* every day in the cafeteria," he says lightly. "Though I'd certainly be flattered if that was the case."

I roll my eyes. "I don't have time for this."

"Whether you have time for it isn't the issue because it's a thing that has happened and is happening, and we should talk about it."

"We're already late," I mutter.

"We're going to talk about this eventually," he says gleefully.

When I flatten my lips and shoot him another look, he drops the subject.

"Are you sure we don't have time for a quick at-home facial?" he asks instead. "I mean, have you seen how Judy Cooper's new hair accentuates the flawlessness of her skin? I asked her about what she's doing, and she wrote down her entire routine for me."

Andy's always been the worst gossip, and with so many students at our school, he makes it a point to meet and schmooze new people, getting close enough to be friendly and learn their secrets while never revealing too many truths about himself.

If he wanted to, Andy could befriend just about anyone and do anything—with the exception of cheerleading, evidently—but that's not who he is. At the surface, his personality is loud and over the top, but it overcompensates for the insecurity he tries to bury so deeply.

It's why we work so well as best friends, regardless of the fact that we seem like total opposites.

He makes a big, funny show of strutting through the entrance, looking handsome as hell in his suit, but the way he squeezes my hand tightly, I know he's internally pleading that this whole night with Michael goes well.

"This is one hell of a turnout," Michael says appreciatively as he steps up to offer me a hug of congratulations. "And you look great."

It's nice of him to make a point to greet me even though it's only been a few hours since we were sitting together in the cafeteria.

"Thank you," I return, noting that he's wearing a blazer and tie. "You do as well."

"And what about me?" Andy asks, arching a brow.

"Oh, you're on a level of existence that 'great' doesn't even begin to describe," Michael answers smoothly, brushing his hand along Andy's bicep.

I definitely don't take offense to that distinction because it's one hundred percent true.

The two of them wander through the crowd—which is probably quadruple the turnout of last year—while I make my way over to the wall featuring my own work.

Mr. Wilde instructed those who submitted pieces to hover around our own space as a reminder to everyone and their wallets that talented students will benefit from their generosity.

I hope one day to feel proud to show off my work, but

standing here, watching people mill around in judgment, I only fidget awkwardly.

A few attendees eye my pictures with interest, but no one stops to chat or ask questions, even when I try my best to smile and come across as welcoming.

The sophomore manning the desk and cashbox has come by other students with a few SOLD! stickers to display on their pieces, but I have yet to receive one.

I scan the crowd, picking out some familiar faces, until my gaze lands on Vince.

So, I guess Andy was right to assume he might make an appearance.

Vince is in the middle of a mass of people, holding everyone's attention with whatever story he's telling.

The few times I've witnessed him speaking to others, he's appeared bored or disinterested, but among the entire lineup of his teammates and coaches, he seems to thrive.

I easily spot Uncle Eric in the throng, along with the mob of freshmen who follow Vince between class periods and brag about attending all of his practices.

Vince is definitely responsible for this turnout, and that realization makes me pinch the bridge of my nose.

Him showing up is a nice gesture, I guess, and some sort of repayment for nearly ruining my photos, but instead of his presence encouraging people who might actually be interested in art and promoting the fundraiser, it's only brought in social climbers who want to fawn over him.

On some level, I understand it.

In my brief analysis of Vince Novak, I've observed his skill at turning the shine on and off, able to focus with tunnel vision on ignoring his surroundings when he wants to—like when the mob gets annoying and he doesn't want to be bothered—or like now, when he's unleashing his charm in full force and taking everything in.

It's to be expected from someone with a future as big and promising as his, just like it was for Jake.

With my brother, however, you always got the high-energy, overbearing confidence whether you wanted it or not.

I lean back against a vacant space on the cool tile wall and force my gaze away from the soccer star.

If Jake were here, he'd be right by my side, peddling my amateur photographs to anyone who would listen.

Then again, maybe if he was still alive, I wouldn't even be here.

Who knows if I would have stayed here after he graduated from college or if I would have willingly given up my daily life to be in his close proximity, just like I had done for so many years.

I almost resent the idea, and it floods me with shame and too much emotion to process in public.

I slip off to the bathroom easily enough, since no one is paying attention to me or my art, and spend a good ten minutes staring at my reflection and mentally willing myself to maintain my composure.

After splashing water on my face, I return to my post, but it's no longer unoccupied.

Somehow, Vince has managed to escape the crowd of people, and he's chosen to spend his reprieve in front of the work he nearly ruined.

His arms are crossed over his broad chest, and he's looking—*really* looking—at my photographs like he's trying to understand how it's all connected or what the deeper meaning is behind each piece.

"You've seen most of these before," I say lightly as I approach.

He nods, not tearing his eyes away. "These are new," he says, pointing to a few recent additions.

I'm a little impressed that he remembers.

"What's this one from?" He gestures to a photo of my own hand that I took when I visited Andy at work earlier this week.

It was a vanilla day, but he still gave me sprinkles just because he wanted to add a little color to the cone. I stood in the last of the summer sun just a little too long, and a line of melted ice cream, dotted with a few green and pink sprinkles, dripped its way down my arm.

This has happened to me many times, of course, as Andy has a way of distracting me with some wild story, but this week was the first time I had the opportunity to capture the moment on film.

"Dream Freeze," I answer.

Vince finally looks at me, wearing a curious expression. "Is that an actual place or a state of mind?"

My lips quirk, but I'm not smiling.

I refuse to do so.

"It's an ice cream shop," I tell him.

"Oh, yeah," he nods. "That's right by North Park, right?"

"Yep."

"Your favorite place?"

He's trying to have a conversation with me.

I'm aware of this.

"Maybe."

Vince laughs at my non-answer. "Well, it's just, I'm new here, and I'm always looking for new...uh, ice cream places."

Even I can't completely stifle a snort at how ridiculous that sentence is.

"Well, I'm sure your freshmen fan club would *love* to show you around town," I say lightly. "They're probably missing you now, actually."

He chuckles. "They're fine on their own. Besides, I'm trying to pick out a photo for my new bedroom."

"Oh, no, that's okay—"

"This one will do," he says resolutely.

He's trying to be nonchalant about it, but it's the picture of the dead bird that he asked me about in the darkroom.

I'm curious as to what about the picture resonates with him.

But I don't ask.

He looks at the price tag on the back. "All that work for only five bucks? Total steal."

I grind my teeth.

He's right.

I don't even know if selling these at such a low price will even cover the materials used to create the pictures, but it's not like every high schooler is flush with enough cash to even consider spending more than that.

"You're not supposed to take them off the wall," I explain as he tucks it under his arm and reaches for his wallet.

He shrugs, like he doesn't live under the same societal norms and rules as everyone else.

"And I can't accept the money myself," I continue. "You'll have to go to the cashier up front."

"Fine," he says, heading that way.

Damn athletes think they can just own the world.

My world, specifically.

"Vince," I say, calling his attention once more.

He turns with a genuine smile on his face that reveals that perfect little flaw.

If he's going to walk into my life and do what he wants without consequence, the least I can do is take something back for myself.

I raise my camera and snap a photo before he's caught up in the crowd once again.

SEVEN

In most situations, I consider myself an observer.

It's not just your standard people-watching that most wallflowers find fascinating. I try to really understand what is happening around me, even consider different backstories and problems, and admire how confident people can be when they aren't aware of being watched.

That's probably why I'm so naturally drawn to photography, along with the fact that it enables me to cave into myself and stay distanced from the world around me.

Like now, as I sit in art class, on my favorite stool by the window, I notice how the room is still buzzing with excitement over last night's event.

Owen's all smiles, congratulating the students on a successful night as he mills around the room, commenting on brushstrokes or offering suggestions for minor adjustments to change the perspective.

I stare out the window, not even pretending to accomplish anything I'm supposed to do today as I wait for him to approach.

When he finally sits down beside me, leaning in so we aren't overheard, he frowns.

"It was a good start," he ventures quietly. "But not enough."

I exhale, trying to force the disappointment to leave my body, but the burden still weighs heavily on my chest. "How short are we?"

"About fifty thousand dollars," he says easily, like that's not a massive amount of money.

"And we have to raise it *ourselves*?" I clarify.

He shakes his head. "If we're able to get a good chunk of it, show there's enough interest in continuing the program, then the board is willing to fund the difference."

"This is ridiculous," I huff, crossing my arms.

"I don't disagree." Owen removes his hat so he can run his fingers through his slightly wavy brown hair. "But as grateful as I am for the company and commiseration, I think it's time for you to stop worrying about it."

I open my mouth to argue, but he waves me off.

"You're just beginning to tap into your art, and you have such a short time left until you graduate and have to deal with your own financial woes. For now, I think you should put all your time and energy into your craft."

He pauses to ensure I'm taking in his words, then asks, "What are you going to work on next in the darkroom?"

"Does that question even matter if it's not going to exist next semester? It'll be turned into a closet to store, I don't know, *shin guards* or something."

"I do actually have some good news for you," he says, pushing past my irritation.

He fishes his wallet from his back pocket, then hands over a pristine white business card.

"What's this?" I ask him.

"I have a friend who owns a studio in Shadyside," he explains. "She couldn't make it last night, but I showed her some of your work last time I visited, and she asked me to give you this. I've been meaning to for weeks and just remembered this morning. They do classes and other events, and she said she'd love for you to come by and check it out sometime. Just give her a call."

"Thank you," I say, completely astonished.

"Mr. Wilde?"

A student beckons him over to look at her in-progress drawing, and he pats my shoulder before leaving my side.

I cradle the business card in my palm like it's made of glass.

This opportunity with someone successful in the art world is like a golden ticket, and I dream of being able to learn more and experience what it's like to even be in a gallery, let alone have work showcased there.

But classes? Events? I can't afford any of that, and my parents definitely won't be willing to cover the cost.

And worse, I'm likely going to lose the little hands-on, practical learning opportunity I have come spring semester. This budget cut means I'll be left to learn from the internet and whatever books are available in the library.

I'm being ridiculously selfish, but I can't help but feel dejected.

Photography and art have become my life raft these past

few years, and I hate that, just as I'm trying to figure out how to move ahead and make it into something more, it's about to be taken away.

Between classes, I fill Andy in on what's going on, and while my best friend is concerned about my favorite class and club ceasing to exist, he's more interested in peppering me with questions about my conversation with Vince last night.

I've already told him the extent of it twice, but he's convinced I'm missing some key details or insights.

"And so then he picked up the picture and walked away with it," Andy says.

"Yes."

"Even though you told him he wasn't supposed to?"

I sigh. "Yes."

"And then—"

"Andy," I say forcefully. "Please stop this. I'm begging you. I can't talk about this any longer."

"What?" he says innocently, leaning back against his locker. "I'm just trying to suss out the situation."

"I think you can consider it sussed," Michael jumps in. "But shouldn't we tell Maren more about the rest of *our* night?"

I give him a look of appreciation, even though Andy, of course, called me right after they parted ways last night, but Michael doesn't know that.

As we walk, eventually, the two of them get caught up in how damn adorable they are together that I am left to my own thoughts as I head to my next class, wracking my brain for ideas to help raise money for the art program and embarrassing myself with what I come up with.

There's absolutely no amount of baked goods I can hawk at a bake sale that will earn fifty thousand dollars.

"Maren?"

I blink, picking up on the annoyed tone of my history teacher who is calling for my attention.

My face grows hot when the students around me turn, ready to watch me make a fool of myself. I sigh loudly as Vince's eyes grow wide, and I realize he's been completely oblivious to the fact we've been breathing the same air in this room since the beginning of the school year.

"Sorry, what was the question?" I ask the teacher in my nicest tone.

"Transylvania," she prompts.

I pause and chew on my bottom lip. "What about it?"

A few people around me snicker, but I honestly wasn't asking to be a jerk.

She doesn't know that, though, so I get to watch her nostrils flare. "Tell me what happened to Transylvania after World War I. What country claimed the land?"

"Oh," I say, trying to recall the reading I did last weekend. "Romania?"

"Why?" she asks.

"Um, a treaty?"

She nods.

It's a lucky guess on my part because my eyes glazed over what seemed like dozens of treaties in our textbook.

"Which one?" she presses, not letting me go easily.

I get she's irritated because I wasn't paying attention, but clearly, I don't know the answers, so she's only setting out to embarrass me.

It's one of my least favorite practices that teachers use

and one I always hope not to be on the receiving end of—but today is just destined to suck, apparently.

"Treaty of Bucharest," Vince pipes up.

"Yes." She grins at him, then shoots me a disappointed glare before turning to her next victim. "Name another treaty that came out of the First World War."

Vince glances back at me, offering the same smile I captured on camera last night.

"Thank you," I mouth.

He nods and returns his attention to the front of the room.

After that entire exchange, I should be on my toes, focusing on the lesson so I can be better prepared, but I'm drained.

I'm grateful Owen gave me a heads up about what's happening, but I'm burdened by the fact that everything is on the cusp of being taken away from me.

I breathe a sigh of relief when the final bell rings.

I've made it to Mrs. Smith's room—early for the *Gazette* meeting this time—with hopes of being assigned something I can shoot over the weekend to distract myself. I'm doodling in my notebook while one of our reporters types away noisily in the back of the room.

"Maren?" Ella says as she and Mrs. Smith approach me tentatively.

Their trepidation is definitely not a good sign.

"Mindy's sick," Ella says, cutting right to the chase. "She's okay now, but she almost passed out after the mile run in gym class today, which means..."

I groan, already knowing where this is headed.

Even being wrapped up in my own problems today, I've

been aware of my surroundings enough to notice the entire boys' soccer team in their jerseys and overheard people making post-game plans.

"I know sports isn't your favorite thing to shoot," Mrs. Smith says with a frown. "But this is a huge game tonight, and we need our own photos."

"I thought I got myself fired from sports coverage after opening day last year?" I recall, offering up my flimsiest excuse.

After the first boys' baseball game last year, Ella had told me politely—despite her frustration with me—that we couldn't publish portraits of players chewing gum and blowing bubbles in the dugout or snapshots of their shoes smeared with grass stains.

Now, she chuckles. "Just please try to take pictures of the actual game this time."

I try to imagine myself standing on the sidelines, capturing the blur of athletes running up and down the field.

It's been years since I've stepped foot in the stadium, and the thought of doing so still makes me physically shudder.

Mrs. Smith and Ella exchange a glance at my hesitation.

"Unless you're *really* not okay with it," Ella says. "Then of course I can understand."

Although it wasn't, and still isn't, true, I can't help but recall Amber's criticism of me, suggesting the reason my photos got published was because people felt bad for me and my situation.

"No," I say, pulling out whatever shred of confidence I have within me. "I'll be fine."

And I really hope I will be.

That resolve earns tight smiles from both of them, and I turn my attention to the task at hand, borrowing a few backup SD cards from our staff storage and double-checking that my battery is full before I set off.

It's almost a relief, having no warning before I have to make my return to the stadium because if I were given time to process, I would have probably talked myself out of following through with it.

Instead, the pressure of not letting down the *Gazette*, and my will to defy Amber's insinuation, pushes me forward.

My student press pass is also a free ticket, letting me bypass the entrance booth—which, by the way, does not look like it needs updating enough to drain the entire art budget—and gives me free rein.

I take a deep breath as my sneakers step onto the grass, letting my feelings hit.

Nostalgia surfaces.

Or maybe it's something deeper, more visceral and less logical.

Whatever the emotion, it's sparked by the combination of inhaling the freshly manicured grass while the lights hit my skin.

My ears pound with the sound of the crowd laughing and talking happily in the bleachers.

It's like I'm stepping into a different version of myself that belonged here once upon a time.

I grip my camera to ground myself in who I am at this moment—the young woman who has struggled to cope with immeasurable pain and by fate or cruelty or just dumb luck is back at the source of it all.

Well, it's not this particular field, team, or even coach that caused my brother to die.

But I spent a lot of time thinking that maybe if he'd injured himself or if he didn't shine so brightly and attract so much attention, maybe he wouldn't have gone off to college and eventually...stopped living.

Thinking like that won't help me get through tonight, though.

I meander toward the sidelines, watching the players warm up and the coaches discuss last-minute strategy.

The game hasn't even started yet, and Uncle Eric is yelling at two defenders who are slacking off in their sets of high-knees, ranting about how they need to protect themselves against injury and not let their teammates down.

He's known to be a hard-ass coach, but he's good at what he does.

I lift my camera and capture some of his more *enthusiastic* comments, along with the angry spit that flies out of his mouth.

He's coached hundreds, maybe thousands, of players over the years, and he's immensely respected among the state soccer program.

When Jake went to college, the university even offered Uncle Eric a spot on the coaching staff, but he refused, saying he loved his current job and that it would take getting hit by a truck for him to leave it.

Even then, I could see him being wheeled toward the bench in a full-body cast, screaming about sloppy footwork.

The players pick up their pace, not wanting to receive any more of their coach's wrath, and I click away, getting some of my artsier shots out of my system before I have to cover the actual game.

I catch Vince in my field of view through the lens, and he smirks in my direction before sprinting after an awful pass by one of his teammates.

Once he has the ball, he starts showing off a little more than he should—whether it's for himself, me, or the crowd, I'm not sure, but I take a few pictures.

"Maren?" Uncle Eric says, pulling my attention to him.

I lower the camera and look at him with my own eyes. "Hi."

"You're shooting tonight?" he asks with a heavy dose of disbelief.

I nod and chew on my bottom lip. "The other photographer called out sick."

"And you're...okay with that?" His voice is so quiet that it's almost delicate, but it's still rough. "This, I mean? Being back here."

I take a deep inhale, feeling somewhat relieved he understands the mixture of emotion swirling inside me.

Every inch of this field has a memory associated with it, and my favorites are of Jake's post-goal celebrations. To most people, the moves probably seemed spontaneous, but he and I spent many Sunday afternoons coming up with different scenarios and correlating dances, usually falling over with laughter as they became more ridiculous.

"I think so," I answer, being totally honest.

Uncle Eric glances around the field, no doubt lost in some memories of his own.

I don't know how he's managed to carry on this entire

time, and it guts me that we weren't in a better place to lean on each other.

I reach out to him, slipping my arm around his waist, even though it's an incredibly personal and soft gesture to offer in this setting in front of all these people.

But he doesn't hesitate to pull me into a hug.

I exhale and let myself fold into my uncle's chest, staying there until my breathing is back to normal and the emotion has been buried deep down once again.

When I open my eyes and glance over his shoulder, I see Vince looking absolutely gobsmacked by the position I'm in.

He lightly taps the closest person on the shoulder and tilts his head in my direction, and his teammate looks over at Uncle Eric and me, frowns, and then apparently explains who I am.

It's not something I've tried to hide in any way, so I'm a little surprised that Vince hasn't figured it out for himself, but I get a front-row seat to watching the reaction roll over his features.

At first, I think it's indescribable, but when I look closer, the surprise is clear.

Then, the understanding.

And, finally, the thing I hate most of all, the pity.

"I think it's time to get coaching," I tell him, finally pulling out of my uncle's embrace.

"Make us look good, okay?" Uncle Eric says with a smile.

"I'll do my best," I promise, then step aside so he can do his thing.

And I do mine.

It turns out the team doesn't need me to make them look good because they do far better than anyone thought they would.

It was supposed to be an intense rivalry game—one that warranted a week of spirit to psych up the team—but it's a complete blowout.

Vince scores three goals and has two assists, and I capture at least a dozen shots that I'm pretty happy with, even though they're not my preferred subject or style.

I do a decent job of losing myself in capturing the game and actually covering it, but I sneak in a few of what I mentally call "my style" of shots—like when the other team's goalkeeper tears off his gloves in frustration or when one of our midfielders tackles another in celebration and accidentally knees him in the balls.

It's hard to find the flaws in a game that is, by most accounts, perfect, but I take my little victories where I can.

EIGHT

"When we play, we play to win," Vince says, chatting easily with one of the city's local reporters.

"Clearly," she retorts with a smile. "When you were up against this team last year at your previous school, the margin of victory wasn't quite as big. What can you attribute to the success we saw out here tonight?"

Vince nods. "The coaching staff here, as I've mentioned before, is incredible, and I'm thankful to benefit from Eric Montgomery's training and playbook. But a large part of it is this team right here—" A few of his teammates whoop, not caring that he's being recorded. "—who have really put their all into pushing us toward the postseason."

One of the assistant coaches grins at the excitement of his players, then fills in some color commentary on Vince's answer before I tune him out.

I'm interested in how this whole process works, with the cameraman, the photographers, and the reporters.

Aside from a clear focus on video, it's really not all that different from what we do at the *Greene Gazette*.

When watching videos or clips online or on the local news channel, everything looks so buttoned-up, refined, but from my vantage point, the magic is ruined a little bit—it's just a reporter with a microphone and a camera pointed over her shoulder, pressing him for soundbites.

I step away from the group and flip through my own photos, mentally bookmarking my favorites to start editing as soon as I get home.

"You get some good shots?" Uncle Eric asks as he approaches.

It's no surprise one of his assistants is playing the role of chaperone to Vince on camera—if I didn't have the history with my uncle that I did, the sound of his raspy voice would make me cringe.

But I find it oddly endearing.

"Want to see?" I ask him.

"Definitely."

He leans against the metal chain link fence beside me, and I hold up the camera, flipping through some of the best shots.

"This one, I almost missed," I tell him, zooming in to show how the goalkeeper missed blocking one of Vince's goals by about two inches.

"Very cool," Uncle Eric says.

I click through a few others, offering up some insight on the angles and how I cued up the shots.

"I can see your talent shining through," he compliments. "These are really great."

"Thank you," I say, beaming just a bit. "This one is one of my favorites."

"It's a great one," he agrees, scrutinizing the image. "But look at the footwork here. If Novak had planted his foot, his aim would have been more on target, and we could have scored another goal."

"Should I remind you that you won the game?" I tease, even though I am very familiar with how important the smallest of details are.

"Well, when you're capturing mistakes from my players, I can't help myself." He chuckles.

I take him through a good chunk of the other photos, stopping right before I get to his spit takes—I know he'll hate those shots, and we're probably low on time before he has to go do a post-game talk with the players.

"Hey," Vince calls for our attention.

I've documented so many variations of Vince today—concentrated on the target ahead, elated after scoring, frustrated with a bad call by the referee—but the version I'm witnessing now has the power to shatter me completely.

I could call it sorrow or sympathy or whatever word sounds better in my mind, but it reminds me exactly who I am, what I've been through, and where I'm standing.

I'm so proud of myself for making it through the entirety of the game without letting my emotions bubble over, but I have to take a deep breath to guard myself against whatever Vince is going to say when he confronts me about what he learned before the game.

Uncle Eric doesn't miss the stiffening of my spine when his new star jogs over, so before Vince slows to a stop, my uncle takes a step forward, acting as a human shield.

"Hey, Coach," Vince says, eyebrows pulling together in surprise. "I was hoping to talk to Maren for—"

"Shower off," he snaps, his voice forceful even after hours of yelling, and tilts his head in the direction of the locker room.

"But—"

"Now."

To my relief, Vince complies.

But I am on the receiving end of a longing look as he obeys his coach's request.

I hold his gaze—probably for a little too long—as he effortlessly moves backward across the field until he turns and disappears out of view.

Uncle Eric turns back to me and clears his throat. "He's a good kid."

"Uh huh," I say noncommittally.

"Had a lot of crappy personal stuff happen in the past year, but he's determined to stay on the right path."

I balk at that sliver of information he dropped in my lap. "What does that mean?"

"Not my place to tell," he says, holding up a hand to stop my inquisition. "Besides, aren't you a member of the press?"

"Oh, come on."

I feel like Andy, who makes it a habit of pushing people for gossip—with far more ease than I'm attempting to now.

My uncle just shakes his head. "Anyway, I should get going," he says a little reluctantly. "You know if I don't bring those boys down a few notches, their egos won't cooperate during practice next week."

I smile slightly at that.

He pats me on the back once, just like I've seen him do with Jake thousands of times, before he heads off.

I don't linger too much longer, but I do note the growing number of people who huddle outside the locker room, waiting for Vince to make an appearance.

Knowing Ella will be excited to see how the shots turned out, I send off a text to let her know I'm heading home to edit the photos, and she can expect updates within the next few hours.

Normally, I'd find somewhere away from my house to edit, but I forgot my charger, and my old computer won't last too long while running the necessary software.

When I arrive home, I dump my belongings on the kitchen table and dig through the pantry for some semblance of dinner—in this case a Pop-Tart—and get to work.

I actually have trouble narrowing the list of my favorite photos to under twenty, but I'm not invested enough that I care which are picked to run, so I take my time editing them all, finding the practice somewhat cathartic.

I force myself to keep an objective eye, but I can't help but notice just how good Vince looks in his jersey when he moves and how the fabric clings to his muscles.

"What's this?" My father's tone is gruff, but there's a hint of surprise to it, too.

I quickly shut my laptop and curse myself for getting so lost in the process that I didn't hear my parents get home.

I should have loaded my arms up with food and made myself scarce before they saw what I'm working on, but there's no turning back now.

"Nothing," I say coolly, not missing the excited gleam in my mother's eyes.

"Did you...go to the game tonight?" she asks me.

I sigh. "Yes," I admit.

Not for the reason they're hoping, though.

Still, she holds out, unable to hide the eagerness in her tone or expression. "Have you been thinking of playing again?"

I shake my head, watching her deflate like a balloon.

That reaction would have once evoked guilt, but it now goes into the void of nothingness, along with their idea of a perfect replacement for the son they lost.

It's her fault, really, for getting her hopes up.

No matter how many times I've said I have no intention of ever playing again and informed them what my true passion is, they don't seem to listen, making it very clear they don't support my "hobby."

The language they're fluent in is rife with statistics, odds, and athleticism, and they don't care to learn or embrace that I'm more interested in what my eye sees than what my body can do.

My parents exchange a glance I recognize as exasperation, and I'm seriously debating running out of the room when my father sits across from me. Usually, if they want to yell, they'll stand, so him joining me at the table is a sign we're going to attempt to have a conversation.

"I know you were thinking of applying to one of those art schools," my father ventures.

This is one of the more egregious points of contention between us when we speak—if we speak at all.

"I *have* applied," I clarify, not bothering to add that there's absolutely no way I can afford it on my own.

They would have paid for Jake to play at any school of his choosing, even if he didn't win a full-ride scholarship—which he did—and I know for a fact they have a college fund set aside for me.

I'm just not sure they'll let me use it.

My father's jaw ticks. "What kind of career do you expect to have as a...nature photographer?"

"I don't want to be a nature photographer," I immediately retort.

"Then what exactly do you want to be?" my mother asks.

I can tell it takes enormous effort to keep her tone even.

"I don't know yet," I admit, much to their satisfaction.

They think my indecisiveness means there's still time to convince me to find something else, not that I haven't figured out exactly how I want to turn my passion into a career.

My mother smiles tightly. "Then there's still plenty of time to get back into—"

"No," I say forcefully, cutting her off. "I'm not going to be a soccer player, or an accountant, or one of the jobs that you understand or want me to do."

"We can't see a path for you to be successful at this, Maren," my father explains. "But to be a professional soccer player, you excel in high school, get scouted, go to college or the MLS, and it all happens from there."

"Like how I became an accountant," my mother recounts for probably the twentieth time. "I went to college, then got an internship, and then I worked my way up to my current job."

That sounds incredibly boring.

I don't love how ambiguous my future is at the moment, but I can't imagine having the next thirty years planned out, either—not that there's anything wrong with that, of course. I just know it's not what I want for myself.

In my quietest moments of self-reflection, I picture myself traveling, exploring the strange countries and towns Jake and I used to hear about while watching Premier League games or World Cup matches.

I want to see as much of the world as I can and document what I see for the sake of posterity or my own sanity maybe.

But if I say it aloud, I'm going to be drilled with questions on how I plan to support myself and monetize my work, and I don't have those answers yet.

It's infuriating that I need to justify this to them, defend myself in ways Jake never had to because he could dribble before he could even walk—at least, that's what he always said, even though, logistically, there's no way for that to be true.

But it's true that his talent surfaced early, and his formative years and entire life plans were based around it, so it guts me just a little bit that our parents embraced their young son's wishes wholeheartedly to someday be a professional soccer player, but they can't extend the same courtesy to their nearly grown daughter.

"Even if you don't see a path," I say slowly, trying to keep my emotions in check, "I can't wrap my head around the fact that Jake's dreams were worthy to support and mine aren't."

They both flinch at the mention of him, which is messed up on so many levels.

His bedroom, located right above our heads on the second floor, is practically sealed off as a shrine to him, but they can't manage to hear his name?

It's sad, really.

But I've stopped trying to help them...or ask for help myself.

As far as I'm concerned, I'm all on my own, and at this point, I'm fine with it.

"Whether you support me or not, this is what I want," I say, gathering up my belongings. "But I really, really wish you would."

I move slowly toward the stairs, waiting to see if either of them has a comment or word of encouragement, but I'm met with total silence.

It's not that I expect them to follow me or even try to repair our relationship, but when I pass Jake's door, I can't help but wonder what else got buried with him.

NINE

"Michael, what are your plans for next year?" I ask.

As a now seemingly permanent part of our daily cheese fry mountain ritual, I've decided to make more of an effort to get to know him—and it's an added bonus that I can use him to deflect my acknowledgment about the lack of my own plans.

I do not, however, appreciate how he strategically placed a plate overloaded with vegetables from the salad bar beside the tray of fries.

"Studying business," Michael says automatically.

It's not the quickness with which he says it but the forcefulness that leads me to believe there's not a doubt in his mind it's the right move for him.

At first glance, he doesn't seem like the exceptionally confident type.

He's more quiet and calculated, content to sit back and watch Andy dominate every situation with his appearance and personality.

"Maybe a minor in entrepreneurship," he adds after a beat. "I have a few options, depending on which classes I end up enrolling in, so I probably won't decide that right away."

"And then will you return to Dream Freeze?"

Andy laughs before chomping loudly on a carrot, like the traitor he is, eating a vegetable during our sacred meal.

Michael shakes his head. "My dad's going to run that place until he croaks."

"Maybe finding out about us will send him into early retirement," Andy says with a shrug.

"One can dream," Michael murmurs quietly before clearing his throat. "I have learned a lot from working there, but I think I want to work for another company before I can even think of having something of my own."

"You're pretty ambitious," I say. "And I mean it as a compliment."

"Thanks," he says with a smile. "What about you? What are your plans?"

"Isn't it obvious?" Andy drawls, gesturing to the camera on the table.

"But there are different kinds of photography she can do," Michael argues.

I flinch, recalling the conversation with my parents. "Yeah."

"What are you leaning toward?" he presses.

"I...don't really know yet. I feel like I still have so much more to learn, and I'm not exactly sure what a 'normal' career path looks like. Or if it's even good enough."

"Oh, please." Andy waves a dismissive hand. "You had

Owen's fancy gallery owner friend impressed by your work enough to pass along a business card."

I glare at him for the mocking use of Mr. Wilde's first name. "But I don't know the terms of said business card exchange. He has been really supportive of my photos, but who knows if she was just doing something nice as a favor to him?"

Andy rolls his eyes. "Well, you won't know until you call her."

I grind my molars because I know he's right.

But it's not like I can do anything about it at this exact moment.

Her card is tucked away for safekeeping between the pages of one of my photography books at home—and those are shoved far under my bed so my parents never come across them.

"Let's talk about you instead," I suggest to my best friend, knowing he's just as uncertain about his post-graduation future as I am.

"Or we could talk about why Vince Novak is staring at you," Andy tosses back.

I sigh as he aggressively chews on another root vegetable and raises a challenging brow.

For someone who is supposed to be my best friend, he's really excelling at increasing my blood pressure today.

With absolutely zero subtlety, Michael immediately turns around to confirm Andy's words. "Or we could talk about why he's coming over."

I groan and pull at the ends of my hair. "Please tell me he's not."

"He most definitely is," Andy says smugly. "Do you want some time alone?"

I grab his hand before he can stand up, digging my nails into his skin. "If you leave me alone here, I'm going to tell Michael what happened last Valentine's Day," I threaten, calling up a mental image of Andy puking up candy hearts outside my car window.

"You wouldn't," he gasps, genuinely offended.

"Oh, I would," I say evenly.

He huffs and wrenches his hand from my grasp but makes no move to leave. "Fine."

"Do I even want to know?" Michael asks, looking between us.

"No," Andy and I answer in unison.

Even without Michael's heads-up, I should have known Vince's presence at our table was imminent, given that every single person in my line of view shifted to look directly at me.

My cheeks grow hot with the attention, and I force myself to breathe slowly.

"Hey," Vince says, approaching the end of our table.

I inhale his citrus scent but don't dare look up, keeping my gaze down so that my hair frames my face as a shield.

"Care to join us?" Andy asks as he scoots over, creating plenty of room.

"I don't think we've met," Vince says politely to my companions as he sits.

I think he expects me to make an introduction, but I don't, choosing instead to glare at my best friend for welcoming this very scrutinized interaction into our lives.

"I'm Michael," he jumps in, smiling kindly. "And this is Andy, Maren's best friend."

"And your boyfriend," Andy adds with a smirk.

Michael grins. "That too."

"And this right here is our cheese fry mountain," Andy explains, proudly showing off the mound of grease that looks comically large beside Michael's vegetable plate. "If you're going to start joining us regularly, you'll need to let us know in advance so we can—"

"Do you need something?" I interrupt, keeping my eyes on my chipped fingernails.

If Vince wants to discuss what he found out last night about the relation between my uncle and me—or worse, give some sort of condolences over my losing Jake—I'd rather get it over with quickly.

"Maren, rude," Andy chides me.

"I prefer 'direct,' actually," I retort.

"Well, whatever it is, I'm also curious," Michael admits to Vince, coming to my defense. "Not that we're not enjoying your visit."

Vince's gaze darts between the three of us, taking in the dynamic, then shrugs. "Thought I'd come over to say hello."

"Well, isn't that thoughtful?" Andy poses.

"Sure," Michael half-heartedly agrees.

I ignore their praises and finally meet Vince's gaze. "Hello," I quip.

He smirks. "Hello."

In my peripherals, I see Andy try and fail to suppress a gigantic grin, like my discomfort is the most entertaining thing on the planet.

"Did you do the history reading last night?" Vince asks me.

It's an innocent enough question, but it's the opener to a conversation I don't want to have.

In fact, not one single interaction between us has been deliberate on my part. Vince Novak invaded my life long before he knew it, and I'm ready for him to leave it. I don't want to further associate myself with him and get these constant, citrus-scented reminders of the sport I've grown to resent and the life that's no longer mine.

I spent so many years being wrapped up in Jake's world that, when he died, I barely pulled myself out of the devastation. It took a long time for me to find myself and embrace my own talents, and I don't have the mental capacity for anything else.

More importantly, I'm just fine living in my own little bubble, free of grass stains and hair ties.

"I'd bet that she absolutely did *not* do her required homework last night," Andy chimes in.

"So, you're not interested in learning about the economic state of our country after World War II?" Vince asks.

"I am," Michael says. "I actually just watched a newly released documentary—"

"Unless there are photographs involved, Maren's not interested," Andy cuts in, trying to keep the conversation on me. "It's a good thing you'll be there to swoop in and save the day again if needed, Vince."

Vince looks at me quizzically, like Andy has just revealed some deep, dark secret about me. "You mentioned that to him?"

"Of course she did," Andy says flippantly.

The last thing I need is for this guy to have the very wrong impression that he's regularly the main topic of our conversations.

"I tell Andy everything," I say in defense.

Vince quirks an eyebrow. "Everything?"

"If you're referencing how you nearly ruined all of her pictures, then crashed her fundraiser, and practically stole a picture of a dead bird, then yes," Andy answers.

"Interesting," Vince says lightly, waiting for my reaction.

"Has she told you about your perfect little—"

"Andy, enough," I snap.

My tone is forceful enough to make him realize he wasn't just close to stepping over the line—he was mid-leap.

He presses his lips together, eyes apologetically wide.

I get what Andy's playing at, but even if he thinks he's helping me by somehow creating a false narrative between Vince and me or showboating me around for attention, I'm not going to play along.

My life, at this moment, feels so uncertain, and he's another disruption.

A very handsome one, though.

"I'm getting out of here," I say to no one in particular, then I grab my camera and my bag and storm out of the cafeteria, feeling the weight of my classmates' stares on my back.

TEN

The temptation to hide in the darkroom for the rest of the day is real.

I know if I do stay in my little sanctuary, my parents will receive phone calls about my absence in class, initiating a string of events that will only induce further headache.

My brain stays in a fuzzy, zombie-like state as I go through the motions of scrolling on social media, then pack up my belongings when the bell rings and make my way to my next class.

I'm dissociated enough from my surroundings that I don't register I'm in the presence of a citrus-scented Vince Novak until he walks in the room and smiles at me.

It's a full, teeth-revealing grin—an uncalled-for gesture, really—that breaks me from my stupor.

Because the sight of his perfect little flaw makes my heart pound in my chest.

It's Vince's fault I'm so off-kilter today. Actually, it's

more than that. He's the reason this year has been so intense for me, at school and at home.

And now he's trying to infiltrate my lunch table.

I don't know what Andy told him after I bolted during lunch, but Vince seems extra smug at the moment, even having the audacity to wink at me before he sits down.

Which means I'm probably going to have to strangle my best friend in his sleep.

The rest of the day blurs by, but because I'm trying so hard to *not* think about Vince, he occupies all my thoughts.

As much as I don't want to admit it, the version of me before my brother died would have been impressed by him. I can picture it now—awed by his talent, wowed by how *hot* he is, excited to get to know him.

Maybe that's why I'm unable to escape him.

He makes me feel nostalgia for something I never experienced.

I'm so jarred by that revelation that I accidentally knock into one of the dozen easels in art club, sending a half-dried canvas tumbling to the floor.

Luckily, it lands face-up, so the paint is intact, but I spend a good chunk of time apologizing to the junior artist. He assures me it's fine, but I'm still a little off-kilter by the time I have to run to Mrs. Smith's room to work on *Gazette* projects.

I've learned that five of my photos are on deck for the next edition of the paper, and the rest will be placed in an online slideshow that Ella offered to help me put together after school today.

When I cross the threshold to the classroom, I'm surprised not to find the usual handful of students, busy with their work on the computers or at a desk. It's just Mrs. Smith and Ella.

And they're clearly waiting for me.

"Hello," I say tentatively before taking a vacant seat in the front row.

They briefly meet each other's gaze, having some sort of silent conversation, before turning to me.

It feels very much like they're hosting an intervention—but for what, I'm not exactly sure.

"Maren," Mrs. Smith starts, forcing her voice to remain even. "I got an interesting email this afternoon."

"Oh?" I breathe.

She nods. "I should probably be discussing this with your parents, but I figured we could start with you."

My jaw clenches, and I wish she'd get on with the point and cut the suspense.

"It was a little surprising," she continues. "In my entire career of teaching and advising this very newspaper, I don't think I've ever received an offer like this. Really, it's a testament to the great work all of you students are producing, and I couldn't be more proud to have a part in it."

She prattles on for another minute before Ella interrupts her.

"*The Pittsburgh Review* wants to syndicate your photos," Ella squeals excitedly, then smooths down her long, black hair, as if she's trying to be more professional.

I blink. "What?"

"*The Review* is asking for permission to use your photos on a regular basis."

"What exactly does that entail?" I ask dumbly.

"It's very unusual for a student to be offered this type of

arrangement," Mrs. Smith admits. "Normally, a photographer would contract with a service, then if a paper wants to purchase the photo, the money is split between the service and the photographer."

Ella takes up the explanation. "But since we're a student-run, academic organization, there are all sorts of legal issues involved, so they reached out to ask if you'd be willing to let them print your work with no payment but full credit in the caption."

I exhale in disbelief.

It's been less than a day since my parents hounded me for justification to pursue my photography, so it's almost too perfect that this opportunity has dropped into my lap. Even though I can't make money from this arrangement now, I know, as a high school senior, getting photos in *any* publication is a great start.

My mind races with opportunities to intern with them in the future or continue submitting my photos—maybe even for payment—on a regular basis down the line.

It's a small thing, but it gives me a ray of hope.

"What do you think?" Mrs. Smith asks.

"I think...that sounds good," I bite my lip and grin.

Ella hands me a mock-up for next week's *Greene Gazette* issue, which prominently features one of the more traditional game shots on the front page.

I take in the pictures of Vince in print, pleased that the colors and the lighting translate well in this format.

And then it hits me.

The Review doesn't want my photos, necessarily—they want my easy access to Vince.

I frown so wholly that my entire body slumps.

"They're taking a gamble on Vince getting famous," I say quietly. "They want my photos now so they have the rights to use them later on."

"You figured it out faster than I did," Ella admits with a slight grimace.

She flips to the feature page, which has a mix of studio shots and my kind of photos from the game last night, and taps her finger on a picture of Vince's post-goal celebration face.

"But they did mention they liked your style. It could be a really fantastic opportunity for you."

She's not wrong.

But *of course* the first real shot I have at making a career of this is tied to the very person I'm trying hard not to like, even if I'm already consumed by him.

In a sense, agreeing to this means using Vince to leverage my standing in this world, but I'm not sure if that makes me any better than the people who regularly fawn over him.

Then again, he's the one who showed up here, inserting himself into my life, my brother's legacy, my damn lunch table.

It's about time I did something for myself.

Even if it's not completely ideal, I have to set my pride and personal feelings aside because I absolutely can't pass up this opportunity.

"You don't have to agree to anything now," Mrs. Smith assures me as the silence drags on.

"No," I say quickly. "I'll do it."

"Great," Ella says with excitement, then turns back to Mrs. Smith. "Do we need anything else, or are we okay to get started?"

"Get started with what?" I ask.

"I'll forward you the email," Ella tells me, already bringing her phone up to do so. "But in addition to home games, they've asked you to cover at least one practice a week to get some variety."

"I've already talked to Eric, and he's fine with it," Mrs. Smith adds. "While I'm not required to notify your parents of this arrangement, since it's not a legal issue, I figured he would be the next best thing. And I did want to get his approval for the access required."

"And what did he say exactly?" I press, genuinely curious.

Mrs. Smith smiles at me. "Just that he's supportive of whatever you want to do and is happy to do what he can to help."

As nice as that is, it's strange to me that we're all in agreement, and no one has bothered to fill in the actual subject of the photos.

"And what about Vince?" The words slip out before I can second-guess them. "Has anyone reached out and asked for his permission?"

"He and his mother filled out a carte blanche media form when they submitted for the transfer to Greene," Mrs. Smith tells me.

"Oh," I say.

Well, at least that spares me the embarrassment of asking a favor of him, but it's a little off-putting that I'm allowed to leverage his existence.

Also, I'll have to spend even more time in his presence and on the field.

That realization makes my palms sweat.

"Well, we should probably get going," Ella says.

I fidget with the strap of my bag. "Going?"

"Unless you have plans already, I thought we could head over to practice together. Today might be a good day to shoot, since it's overcast outside."

Most people might assume it would be better to take outdoor pictures on a bright, sunny day, but that's actually not the case—the clouds do an excellent job of diffusing the right amount of light from the sun, giving everything a near-perfect hue.

I consider her offer, knowing full well that, even if I had plans, they'd likely involve taking photographs elsewhere, so I might as well do this now.

"There's no better day than today to start your career as a professional photographer," Ella singsongs, nudging my elbow with hers.

I blink, letting the weight of her words sink in before I stand up. "Let's do this," I say on an exhale, watching both women smile at my enthusiasm.

Ella and I walk side by side over to the practice field, chatting easily about assignments and plans after graduation.

Normally, I'm content to sit back and let others dominate the conversation, but there's something about her that gets me to open up.

I think it's because she's had plenty of practice interviewing faculty and the occasional school board member about topics for the paper, so she's good at getting people to talk.

It's no surprise, really, that she has big plans to be one

of those hard-hitting investigative reporters who uses her skills to dethrone corrupt businessmen and expose grimy politicians—although, I probably shouldn't lump my lack of social graces in with that group.

But even though Ella has a plan in place, she's not fazed by my own lack of one, instead assuring me that plenty of freelance photographers are needed in all industries, and I'll do just fine.

That's part of the reason I've always liked her—not only for her kindness and unwavering support but also because she's so incredibly confident in her belief that everything will work out. It's kind of hard not to agree with everything she says.

I wrap my camera strap around my wrist and eye the field.

The players are running through a series of conditioning exercises, weaving around cones as they sprint. I have renewed appreciation for the fluidity of their movement as I watch them.

I pop off a few test shots, ensuring my settings are in place.

"No photos," one of the assistant coaches calls to me.

Vince, waiting for his turn to run the cones, turns and smiles when he realizes it's me.

"It's okay," Uncle Eric says loudly. "I approved this."

And we get no further questions.

I spend most of the practice out of the way, taking shots from a distance, but as the team switches to a different set of drills, I'm able to get closer without disrupting them.

The tricky part of having human subjects instead of inanimate objects is there's a noticeable shift when they know they're being watched. Instead of going on with their easy, unquestioned existence, they demonstrate a natural inclination to pose or look "better," which actually ruins the picture because their demeanor comes across as forced and strange.

So, in a way, it's kind of a good thing that Vince is comfortable showing off on the field. With a ball at his feet, it doesn't matter if he has an audience of zero or thousands.

And his cockiness is justified.

He's *that* good.

I'm trying to stay objective as I snap photos of the team, but Vince is an easy target, confident in every step and dribble. The ball is merely an extension of him, and he's totally in control as he megs one of the defenders—passing the ball to himself between the player's feet—in a quick scrimmage.

As they wrap up with a final talk from the coaches, Ella asks to see some of my shots, so I flip through the spread while she gushes over them.

"Get any good ones?" Vince asks, bobbing a bottle of Gatorade in his hand as he approaches us.

"Are you kidding?" Ella says. "Maren took them, so of course they're good."

I nod at her in gratitude. "Thanks."

"And she got a really good opportunity today," she continues, surprising me by how she dives right into divulging this information to him. "*The Review* wants to syndicate her photos, asking her to cover games and practices."

"Are you okay with that?" I ask him quickly. "After all, you're what they want, not my photos, really."

He mulls it over, leaving me fidgeting in nervousness.

"Better you than some stranger," he says eventually.

"I guess that's a ringing endorsement," I say nonchalantly, slipping off my bag and bending down to drop my camera inside.

"Great!" Ella exclaims. "And, Vince, we're still on for tomorrow?"

"I hope so," he teases. "Mom made a huge fuss about wanting me to get a new tie and everything."

She laughs. "Well, you're a shoo-in for Homecoming King, so you'd better look the part."

"I'm more concerned over what my sister is going to think about our color coordination," Vince says. "She keeps texting me to remind me how her prom date got the wrong type of flowers, and their pictures are forever ruined."

"Amateurs," Ella says with an exaggerated eyeroll.

I swallow and zip my bag with shaky hands, listening to them flirt so easily and shamelessly.

I tell myself I'm jealous because no conversation—with anyone besides Andy—has ever flowed that easily for me and not because they're apparently going to Homecoming together.

On a *date*.

I jolt upright, standing too quickly, and the movement makes me a little light-headed.

"Are you okay, Maren?" Ella asks, grabbing onto my arm when I wobble.

Nervous laughter bubbles up in my throat. "Totally

fine," I say, voice a little higher than normal. "I'll see you later, Ella."

I walk away as quickly as I can, leaving them to chatter on about things like corsages and limos and slow dancing and whatever else people who have dates to dances do.

I don't know what I thought about my interactions with Vince up until now, but I'm suddenly certain that I've somehow misread every single one of them.

My level of disappointment surprises me.

And worse, I'm still irritated with my best friend, so I can't even drown my sorrows in free ice cream.

ELEVEN

"I've decided you're done being annoyed with me," Andy announces as he walks into my bedroom.

"Good for you," I mutter, keeping my gaze focused on my computer screen.

I have a very high tolerance for his antics, but he knows that Vince is a huge sticking point for me—the mention of his name was enough to irk me for years, and now he's slowly becoming a formidable presence in my life.

I have to tie myself to Vince Novak for the rest of the season because I can't give up such a good opportunity with *The Review*.

It would be *really* nice to have my best friend on my side for all of this, but he seems to be too entertained by my conflicting feelings about Vince to make room for anything else.

"And you're coming with me to a party tonight," Andy adds casually.

Except for stupidity.

"You're joking, right?" I say flatly, finally looking at him.

He falls onto the bed beside me. "Michael got us an invitation to Judy Cooper's house, and *everyone* is going to be there."

"Hard pass."

"Oh, come on, Maren. The alternative is...what? Sitting here by yourself for the zillionth Saturday night in a row?"

"Well, usually, I have plans with my *best friend*," I snap, deflecting the hurt.

He rolls his eyes. "It really wouldn't kill you to be a little social."

"Social is one thing, but going to a Homecoming after-party with you, where you'll promptly ditch me for Michael, is another story altogether."

Andy sighs. "Does the thought of having fun really scare you that much?"

Any retort I could utter falls off the tip of my tongue because I realize it absolutely *does* scare me.

The thought of putting myself out there, actually *being* somewhere and participating in something instead of photographing it, makes my throat want to close up.

My simmering irritation and anger peter out, and in their place is something between shame and embarrassment.

I blink rapidly, trying to will the wetness forming in my eyes to go back to wherever it came from, and swallow the emotion in my throat as best I can.

Andy gasps, taking in my expression. "Oh, shit. It does, doesn't it?"

I run my fingertips over the edges of my quilt, trying to compose myself enough to speak. But my swirling patterns on the fabric stop suddenly when Andy sits up and pulls me into his arms.

"I'm sorry," he says quietly.

Nodding my head, I sink into him, though it almost hurts to be comforted like this—and it's not just because Andy is the boniest human I've ever known.

Best friends are like mirrors, showing the parts of yourself you can't see, and right now, I don't like my reflection.

When Jake died, I internalized so much to stop the hurt, and since then, I've been so intent on keeping a barrier in place from the rest of the world to keep protecting myself.

In many ways, my camera serves as a shield, cutting me off from living my life to instead document the way others live theirs.

Even now, the entire student body is probably at the Homecoming parade, laughing and enjoying the festivities before they all rush home to get ready for the dance. I'm merely speculating, though, because I never actually got around to experience that for myself.

And now, as Andy sits with me silently, I've just had the realization as to why.

I've let fear of opening up, of being vulnerable, of feeling *anything*, really, control my life.

And it's not just sad.

It's mortifying.

Most of all, Jake would be absolutely ashamed of my behavior these last few years.

I sit up abruptly, taking Andy by surprise. "Let's go to that party."

His eyes widen. "We don't have to," he says sweetly. "We can just stay in."

"No," I say resolutely. "We're doing this."

He takes a breath and warily eyes me, likely looking for the cause of the change in my mood. "You're sure?"

I can tell he's tempering his excitement on my behalf. "Positive."

Andy smiles and renews the embrace, but this time, it's one of excitement instead of comfort.

"But, for the record," I say, pulling back, "I'm still a little bothered by the whole cafeteria scene with Vince yesterday."

He chuckles. "Fair enough. But I don't think he was too bothered by it. He just looked happy to be in your presence, and he even stayed after you left."

I hum, unsure of what else to say.

I've already let my feelings come close to spilling out tonight, and I don't want to tell Andy about how shocked I was at the news of Vince and Ella going out for fear he'll want to dissect every little detail with me.

I grind my teeth at the thought of how off guard—and other emotions I force myself not to name—I was by that news.

"Let's get started," Andy says, standing up with purpose.

The rest of the afternoon passes by like we're stuck in a teen movie montage. We get greasy takeout food, then spend a fair amount of time pampering ourselves with manicures, pedicures, and those sheet face masks that make me feel like I'm in a horror movie.

Andy loves every single second of it, filling the day with gossip about our classmates, his family, and random celebrities he follows online.

Around dinnertime, we order in and watch a movie, remaining huddled on my bed until Michael texts Andy to say they've just announced the final song at the dance.

So, finally, after a day of anticipation, I change into a pair of Andy-approved jeans and a black, off-the-shoulder top. Then after a quick stop at his house so he can throw on a button-down, we're off.

"Aren't people going to be really dressed up?" I ask him on the ride over. "While we just look like...this?"

Andy taps on the steering wheel to the beat of the music. "Michael said most people change as soon as they get to the party."

"Makes sense," I admit. "I still can't believe you're okay he went with someone else."

"Who is *female*," Andy reminds me. "Besides, how many times have I asked you to go with me?"

"But I've always said no," I retort.

"That's not the point. The point is that it's not like going to a dance means you're married to someone. Plenty of people just go to dances, and it doesn't really mean anything of—" Andy stops talking, eyes darting around like he's seeing the answer to a problem work itself out in front of his eyes.

"Don't say it," I beg him.

Andy presses his mouth shut, and from his side profile, I can see the strain it takes for him to keep his mouth closed.

When we idle at a stoplight, he finally turns to me.

"I wonder if Vince Novak will make an appearance tonight," he says innocently, as if he were making a comment about the weather.

"I don't," I say quickly. "Wonder, I mean."

Andy chuckles as he presses the gas pedal, navigating us into one of the many neighborhoods in our town. "Maren, you're many things, but a liar isn't one of them."

I close my eyes, wanting to see absolutely none of whatever look is on his face.

Thankfully, before I know it, we stop in front of a gigantic house. We get out of the car, and I take in the chaos before us. The party appears to be in full swing, with people milling around on the front lawn holding red cups.

"So, no one's parents care that everyone here is drinking underage?" I ask Andy as we approach the keg that's set up on the porch.

He waves to a few people he knows before answering my question. "Judy Cooper's parents are gone for the weekend."

I gesture to the other houses on the street, all of which sit only a few hundred feet away from the speakers blaring pop music. "But...neighbors?"

"Is this your idea of having fun?" he teases. "Spending the entire night worried someone's going to call the cops on us?"

"I didn't realize I'd have to trade logic and what's *legal* to have fun," I retort.

He hands over a cup of warm beer.

I can't help but grimace at how stale it smells, but I take a tentative sip, finding it's not even a little bit better than I imagined.

Honestly, I don't know how Jake used to drink this stuff all the time—it's gross.

"Hey there," Michael says, greeting Andy and me.

"Having fun?" Andy asks.

Michael smiles slowly, and I notice how flushed his cheeks and neck are.

"I am now," he slurs slightly.

Andy shakes his head. "Well, you're already swaying, so let's head inside."

I awkwardly follow, playing third wheel and gripping my beer like it's my ticket inside.

We pass through a group of people dancing in the entryway, then through a more casual setup of card games in the living room before we come to a stop in the kitchen.

Michael and Andy integrate flawlessly with the group there, but I hang back, taking another gulp from my cup just so I have something to do.

I admire Andy for many things but especially for his lack of self-consciousness.

I don't know how people are so comfortable in these types of situations—not just at a party but anywhere in large crowds.

All I can do is overanalyze the situation, take in the different angles at which people hold themselves, pay attention to how they react, and study their movements.

I wish I hadn't taken Andy's advice to leave my camera behind because I'm itching to capture the scene in front of me—sticky countertops, smeared makeup, easy laughter.

It's probably for the best, though, that I'm not responsible for documenting teenage drinking, so I'm stuck in observation mode without a way to make the image permanent.

Andy glances over his shoulder without breaking stride

in his current interaction and reaches his hand out for mine, attempting to pull me into the conversation.

It's a nice gesture, but I feel a little pathetic, like he's trying to show me off or something.

I don't need him to literally hold my hand at this party, urging me to make an effort to socialize.

Honestly, getting here was the only goal I had for tonight, so if Andy decided at this very second that he was done, I would happily head back home.

"Come on, Maren," he says, wiggling his fingers in my direction.

"I'm okay," I tell him with a look that reassures him to let me slip out through the kitchen door and into the backyard.

Given that the house is on the larger side, I'm surprised at how small the space out back is. There's just enough room for a small grill, a table, and a few sets of chairs in the grass.

But at least it's quiet.

I inhale the fresh October air and take a seat, kicking my legs up and leaning back to stare upward at the sky.

I wish I knew the names and positions of all the constellations, but part of me is happy to live in ignorance. The randomness of them kind of makes it more appealing, honestly…like the most beautiful things in my line of sight are just as disheveled as I feel.

Out of all the things I've captured through my lens, I've never successfully taken a picture of the night sky, so this is a good reminder to do more research to see what equipment or settings I'll need to do so.

The back door slides open, creaking slightly in the silent night.

"I'm fine, Andy," I call out, keeping my gaze fixed upward.

When I don't get a response, I turn, expecting to see him in all his well-socialized glory, but of course, it's not my best friend stepping toward me.

It's Vince Novak.

And he's wearing a dark gray suit.

"Oh," I exhale, then I swallow another gulp of beer, hoping it will numb my senses.

His expression is indecipherable as he sits down across from me. "I didn't see you at the dance," he says.

"You were looking for me?" I ask it so quickly that my curiosity could be taken as eagerness.

I cringe and place my cup on the table because I, apparently, don't need any additional liquid courage to get through the night.

"Yes," he says simply. "I was."

I meet his dark gaze, noting how the light from the kitchen window casts a shadow on his features.

My fingers itch to capture the severity of it.

"Why?" I ask.

He leans forward, resting his elbows on the table between us.

His eyes rake over my appearance, lingering on the exposed skin of my shoulders and collarbones, and my heart pounds.

"I really need to explain why I've been trying to talk to you?" he asks softly.

"Yes," I say immediately.

Vince's forehead wrinkles, but I don't falter.

"What did you want to discuss?" I press.

The alcohol is helping my mind admit that I'm desperate to understand if all these weird run-ins, and his sudden change in lunch plans, are the result of any of my family members—living or dead—or because of me.

His stony facade cracks, and he swipes my cup, taking a large drink of my beer.

As he grimaces at the taste, I realize the gesture is a distraction from my words, as if he needs time to process my question.

And for the first time, it occurs to me that I, of all people, somehow make *him* nervous.

"That's disgusting," he says, placing the cup between us again.

"Yes."

"I don't know how people drink that stuff."

"What did you want to talk to me about, Vince?" I ask the question somewhat forcefully, trying to latch onto the confidence he usually possesses and hoard it for myself.

"I want to get to know you," he answers seriously.

"But why?"

He lets out a frustrated laugh. "What do you mean why?"

"You didn't seem interested in talking to me before you found out I'm Jake Montgomery's sister," I say coolly, finding the words aren't as painful to say as I thought they would be.

"Not true," he counters immediately. "But...everything kind of makes sense now."

I chew on my bottom lip, mulling over his words.

I'm distant, a little broken, and socially awkward because of what I've been through, and everyone, including him, can see it. I've known that for a while, but somehow, it hurts more to hear him acknowledge it aloud.

I should get up and leave, track down my best friend to help distract me, but I'm rooted in my seat.

"So, why didn't you come to the dance?" Vince asks, changing the subject slightly.

"Not my thing," I say.

He nods. "Well, you didn't miss much."

"You and Ella didn't have a good time?"

"Considering she ditched me to go FaceTime her college boyfriend about fifteen minutes in, and I had to spend the rest of the evening dodging that mob of freshmen, I'd say it wasn't on my top-ten list of best school experiences ever."

I don't bother hiding the confusion on my face.

Vince's smile slowly spreads on his face as he takes me in.

"Ella and I are just friends. We have been forever." He shrugs off his jacket, getting more comfortable. "Our sisters are really close. They used to go to the same dance class every Tuesday night, and Ella and I would sit, bored out of our minds, while they practiced. She wanted to go to the dance, a last high school hurrah with her friends, so she asked me as a favor so she wouldn't have to pose in the group pictures alone."

"That's…" I'm trying to find a word that seems appropriate but doesn't give off the vibe I'm overly invested in the explanation. "Nice, I guess."

Vince rolls up his sleeves, not even looking at me.

"Besides, it's not like going to a dance means you're married to someone."

Those words seem eerily familiar.

After a beat, I place them, and my gaze snaps toward the kitchen window just as Andy backs away from it.

"I'm going to murder Andy," I say through clenched teeth.

Vince laughs. "Or, instead of turning to violence, maybe you and I could just hang out?"

"Hang out," I repeat.

"Yeah, like you can tell me more about yourself and your photography, and you can ask me whatever you want to know."

I take a deep breath, trying to regain some of my footing. "Who says I want to know anything about you?"

He rolls his eyes. "Says Andy."

"What about me?" my best friend asks as he steps through the back door.

I'd be willing to bet my entire college fund that he has spent the last twenty minutes eavesdropping on our conversation, waiting for the perfect spot to jump in.

"Nothing," I grumble.

"Well, Michael's sick," Andy announces. "I'm going to take him home."

I stand up to join him, but he waves me off.

"You should stay here," he suggests. "I'm sure Vince would be happy to get you home."

Vince nods. "Of course I'll—"

"What kind of friend would I be if I let Andy hold back Michael's hair all on his own?" I jest, grateful to have an excuse to get back to my bed to process everything I just learned.

"I've got it, Maren, honestly," Andy insists, widening his eyes in obvious encouragement for me to stay behind.

I loop my arm through his, and before either of them can argue, I pull Andy back inside through the throng of people who can allow themselves to simply enjoy the moment.

TWELVE

I swear, I can *feel* things changing.

Every year, it's the same—one day, I'm clinging to my short-sleeved shirt like it's keeping me alive, and the next, I'm diving headfirst into my coziest sweater and stepping into a pair of boots.

But it's not just the weather; although, I think that's partially to blame.

At lunch, Andy declares, moving forward, we're going to be eating hoagies on Mondays instead of french fries, just to mix it up.

I've had enough change in recent years—hell, in recent days—to last me a lifetime, but even I know this is too trivial an issue to argue, so I take a bite of the overlarge sandwich and don't even bother complaining when breadcrumbs flake all over the place.

"Here," Michael says, offering me a napkin.

"Thanks."

It's a futile effort, but I do take more care in my next

bite to make sure the mess goes on the table instead of my lap.

"There's also this," Michael adds, sliding today's edition of *The Review* across the table.

Anticipation floods my system as I carefully flip back to the sports section, trying not to wrinkle the thin pages.

I've been submitting photos to the local paper's online file sharing system, but I haven't heard back on whether they like what I've sent over or when they're going to be published.

My hands shake slightly as I finally reach the correct page, but I frown, not seeing my name or photos anywhere.

Michael clears his throat. "Second page of the news section."

I quirk an eyebrow at him, then follow his suggestion.

The article is small compared to the others on the page, but the headline stuns me:

Greene to Lose Arts, Advanced STEM Programs in Budget Cuts

"Guh," I groan.

If anything, I could be a little reassured that it's not just the arts that the school board wants to dismiss, but I'm truly heartbroken to see this news in print.

The reporter details attending a school board meeting, then dives into some of the specifics regarding percentages and revenue from the athletic teams, along with a bunch of other statistics that make my mind swirl in confusion.

Because no matter what the numbers say, I don't understand how cutting back on actual academic-based curriculum is even an option.

"What's this?" Andy asks, nodding to the paper as he

dumps a few bags of chips from the vending machine on the table.

I hold it up so he can see over my shoulder, but he promptly crumples it up and tosses it into the garbage can.

"Hey," Michael protests. "I wasn't finished."

"Join the twenty-first century and read on your phone," Andy retorts as he slides down beside him.

"Do I need to remind you that you happily bought me a copy of *The Review* nearly every day this summer?" Michael shakes his head in exasperation. "Not to mention your best friend is expected to get her first professional photo published in that very same paper, and you're telling me now is the time to break my print-based preferences?"

"My best friend is actually shattered right now because her favorite class and club is—"

"Stop," I plead, rubbing my temples.

"Sorry, I didn't mean to bring you this news and then give you a headache," Michael says.

"It's fine," I tell him. "I'm going to figure out a solution."

"Because it's clearly up to a seventeen-year-old to solve a budgeting crisis that adults with years of experience can't sort out on their own," Andy drawls.

"Try not to be too helpful, here, Anderson," I snap at him.

"Helpful with what?" Vince asks.

I meet his gaze as he drops his books and a brown paper bag on the table, then sigh as he takes the seat beside me.

"There was an article this morning about the budget cuts for the arts program," I explain.

Vince grimaces. "I'm sorry."

"It's not like you're directly responsible," I reply, shaking it off. "But I was just saying that I need to think of another idea to raise more money to keep the program."

"The fundraiser didn't help?" Vince asks.

I press my lips together. "Not enough."

"What about...organizing a walkathon or doing some sort of talent show to raise money?" Michael suggests.

"You're dealing with art students," I remind him gently. "Most of us are cripplingly introverted, afraid to even show off our own work, let alone do an athletic activity or coordinate with people to put on a gigantic event."

Andy snorts, likely mentally picturing some of the more artistic students jogging around.

"The art show is like pulling teeth as it is," I continue. "And all they have to do is submit their work and stand beside it for a few hours."

"So, we have a bunch of people who can paint, draw, and take photos," Vince says, eyeing my camera on the tabletop. "What if you offered to do headshots or portraits for people?"

"What if you just took your shirt off and let Maren photograph you?" Andy teases.

Vince blinks, then breaks out one of his signature smiles. "That's it."

"Oh no," I say, shaking my head vigorously. "Not happening."

"Totally agree," Vince adds quickly. "But I think I've come up with a solution to get these damn goalposts *and* save your little art club."

"Don't patronize me by calling it 'little,'" I say evenly.

"I just meant it's endearing."

"Right, because it's just so *cute* that you guys run around in your little knee socks—"

"You know that's not what they're called," Vince tosses back, then stops, letting the sound of Andy's laughter fill the gap as he takes a deep breath. "But yes, I understand your point, and I apologize."

I open and close my mouth a few times in surprise, then clear my throat. "Right. So what is your actual idea?"

"Well, my sister's old dance school sold calendars to raise money when they needed to redo the floors in the studio," Vince explains. "They had to hire a photographer, which cost them money, but we already have one of those."

"You think we should take pictures of everyone's work and sell it in a calendar format?" I ask, skeptical.

Vince shakes his head. "We should join up with the soccer team and the art club to create backdrops and take photos. That way, we can leverage the soccer team's fan base to sell more."

"That's...not a terrible idea," I admit. "You think this would be approved by the team?"

"Well, I do know someone who has pull with the coach," Vince deadpans.

"Let's crunch some numbers," Michael says, pulling out his phone.

We all lean in as he opens the calculator.

"So, let's say you do a run of a thousand calendars. Since you're bulk ordering, you'll pay about five dollars to print. If you sell them for thirty dollars and split the prof-its...you're looking at a ton of money. Enough to make a dent and prove the arts are worth saving."

"Well, damn," Andy says, crunching on a potato chip with a smirk on his face.

"What do you think, Maren?" Vince asks.

I bite my lip in thought.

It's a brilliant idea, really—the perfect combination of the more commercial appeal of the soccer players with the artistic eye of the art club.

"I'll run the idea by Mr. Wilde and see what he thinks," I say finally. "Then I'll talk to Uncle Eric."

"Let me know if you want me to be there when you do," Vince offers. "But I would ask for one stipulation to the agreement you're going to pitch."

I eye him curiously. "What's that?"

"The profits we set aside for the soccer boosters should be split equally between the boys' and girls' teams."

Andy glances at me, so I keep my expression neutral. "Oh?"

"As contentious as funding seems to be outside of the athletic department, it's even worse within it," Vince explains. "The girls' team hasn't gotten new uniforms in at least two years, and we have multiple kits."

"I know," I scoff before I think better of it.

Vince blinks. "Right, you probably have to listen to discussions about these things all the time," Vince says.

"I know because I played," I admit quietly.

Vince blinks. "You did?"

"She didn't just play," Andy says dramatically. "She dominated."

I think it's a little bit of an overstatement, but I don't refute it because I know I was good.

It was impossible not to be, really, given how Jake's

talent was utterly out of this world, so it was inevitable that I'd pick up some of his skills over the years I practiced with him in our backyard under Uncle Eric's watchful eye.

"Really?" Vince asks, seemingly impressed.

I shrug. "It's been a while, though."

Andy watches me chew on my bottom lip, and before I can deep dive into my memory bank, he pivots our topic of conversation slightly.

"So, let's say this project gets approved by both parties. Who should be on the short list for each calendar slot?" he asks, pulling out a notebook to jot down ideas.

We spend the remainder of lunch planning, coming up with themes and general ideas, and discussing which players would be the best fit for each month.

It's a fun exercise, and I like seeing how into planning this Andy is—he has opinions and suggestions for every slot.

When the bell rings, signaling the next period, I walk to art with a firm grip on the paper containing Andy's notes and Michael's price projections, feeling more confident about approaching Mr. Wilde with the idea now that some of the planning is done.

"Maren, wait up," Vince calls, jogging until he reaches my side.

As we round the corner together, I notice our classmates' stares following our movements. I try as best I can to block them out.

"What's your next class?" I ask him.

"Anatomy," he answers.

The science wing is in the opposite direction of the art room, but I don't call him out on it.

After all, he is once again using the notoriety that comes with his presence to help me out.

The least I can do is not state the obvious.

"Thank you again for your idea," I say.

"It's really no problem," he assures me. "It sounds like it will actually be pretty fun."

"Even so, I appreciate it."

I feel a little guilty at my long-held, outright hatred of his existence when he's been nothing but kind toward me since he arrived at Greene.

Which reminds me...

"There's something I wanted to ask you about," I say to him.

He shoves his hands in his pockets as we walk. "Yeah?"

"Why did you move here?"

I see a flash of something I can't place cross his features, but he catches himself and puts on a neutral expression.

"I wanted to be coached by the best and have a shot at winning—"

"I don't buy that," I interrupt him. "I know that's the answer you always give, but I don't think it's the truth."

He shrugs, feigning nonchalance. "It's the right answer."

I stop moving, even though we're across the hallway from the art room.

Vince's gaze drops to his shoes.

He's hiding something.

And he seems to feel ashamed of the fact.

"It's fine," I say gently, even though I'm a little disappointed. "You don't have to tell me."

He swallows and nods, finally meeting my eyes once again.

"Maren?" Mr. Wilde's voice cuts through the noise of the hallway. "You okay?"

I turn to him, offering a smile as the bell rings, and after one final glance at Vince, I take a breath and head into the classroom.

"Good luck," Vince calls behind me.

I appreciate the send-off because I think I'm going to need all the luck I can get.

THIRTEEN

I get immediate buy-in from Mr. Wilde.

But it takes me a week to get some time with Uncle Eric, and his agreement comes after I corner him following a cold afternoon practice.

Then it's another two weeks to coordinate everyone's schedules, which barely gives the art students time to finish their contributions to the project.

I also have to get permission from Mrs. Smith to use her classroom for non-*Gazette* related activities, but she seems thoroughly entertained by the idea, saying she's glad to have someone as scrappy and resourceful as me considering a future career in journalism.

I don't bother to correct her that I really don't have plans for that at the moment.

Now, we just need to prove our case with cash.

And a lot of it.

Finally, on a perfectly chilly fall Friday, Andy and I are frantically trying to coordinate everything before the players arrive. He's in his element, thriving under the pressure of organizing all the art pieces and backdrops that we'll need to quickly clip up before the shots.

All I want to do is hide behind my camera, focus on my singular role, but Andy doesn't let me fade into the background. He puts me right to work, making me line up athletes as they arrive and give the rundown of what to expect.

Someone turns on music and opens a window, letting in a light breeze that is the perfect temperature to offset the heat from the lights and all the people.

Once Andy proclaims it's time to get started, the goalies from both teams pose in their long-sleeve jerseys and gloves.

One of the junior painters created a backdrop where it looks like a giant snowman made of soccer balls is coming for them, and I capture a few funny shots of the group with their stern game faces on, ready to pounce in protection of their net.

For February, we feature a couple—a defender and a midfielder from the girls' team—who holds a somewhat lopsided ceramic heart made by a very enthusiastic freshman.

The months continue parading on, blurring together in a whirl of color, wide smiles, and different props.

I expected everyone would want to get out of school once their turn finished, but most of the models remain, whooping and laughing to encourage their teammates to open up in front of the camera.

It's not until the November shoot is set up that I realize how much I'm enjoying this whole endeavor. After working solo for so long, I kind of like operating as a team and working toward a common goal while also challenging myself with all the different personalities and settings.

For December, Vince barrels in the room dressed as Santa, and the captain of the girls' team is dressed as Mrs. Claus. They pose adorably under a ridiculously large, wire mistletoe, but he keeps complaining about how itchy the fake beard is while she whines about the heels Andy forced her to wear.

"Take them off," I suggest. "And toss them to my feet."

They both grin and follow my instruction as I shoot, flash flickering in repetition.

It might be my favorite set of pictures—the two of them in fits of laughter as the pieces of their costumes fly toward the camera.

"And that's a wrap," Andy yells to the room, flipping off the studio lights.

Everyone in the space applauds at the success.

I take a deep breath, giving myself the length of one long inhale and exhale to take it all in before we start to dismantle the set.

Most people are eager to help, chatting easily with one another as they do, but once it's just Andy and me, he collapses dramatically at a desk, waving his hand in front of his face, like he's completely out of steam.

I, on the other hand, feel exhilarated as I sit beside him and flip through the last round of shots, pleased with how they turned out.

"Look at this one," I squeal for the dozenth time.

"Maren, I'm over it," he says, sliding down in his chair.

"I don't care if you took the greatest photo in the history of all photography, I can't look at another one."

"Fine," I huff.

Vince returns after changing back into his normal school clothes, bypassing a group of his friends who are waiting in the hallway.

"Hey, guys," he says to us with a grin. "A bunch of people are going over to Bill's tonight. Want to come?"

"Under normal circumstances, I'd never say no to a party, but after this…" Andy gestures around the room that's back to normal. "I want nothing but a long soak in the bath and a face mask."

"Fair enough," Vince relents. "Maren?"

His dark brown eyes plead with mine, but I know enough about soccer parties that I want to steer clear of them for the rest of my life.

"I think I'll pass," I tell him. "But thanks."

"It'll be fun, though," he presses. "We could play cards or watch a movie or whatever."

He seems so hopeful that it almost hurts to turn him down, but I do it anyway.

I shake my head. "I'm just going to get something to eat, then go home."

"Okay," he says quickly, then turns away, following his friends out the door.

I am a little surprised he let it go so quickly, but I chalk it up to reading a little too much into our interactions.

Andy merely shrugs at his behavior, then we both do a final scan of the room, ensuring everything is where we found it before we lock the door behind us.

I give my best friend a big hug and a round of thanks in

the parking lot before he heads off, mumbling about whether his boyfriend will be kind enough to drop by later with some ice cream or fast food.

"So, where are we going?"

Vince's voice hits my ears the moment my hand touches my driver's side doorhandle.

"What?" I ask, turning around to see him approach.

"Well, you didn't exactly offer a formal invitation, but I could eat," Vince says. "And since you're hungry, too, why not join forces?"

I bite back a smile.

I shouldn't be this pleased at how smooth he is.

"I'm buying," he insists. "It's the least I can do for you making me look so good in photos all the time."

"You know, bribery doesn't work on most girls," I tell him.

He raises his hands defensively. "It's not—"

"But I'm not most girls," I finish, letting my grin spread.

"Good," he says, his expression mirroring mine. "What are you in the mood for?"

I shrug. "I'm not really picky."

"Neither am I," he says. "I'm still new to the area, though, so I'll defer to you on what's best."

I consider the running mental list of my favorite options. "Well, I think I have a place in mind that has a little bit of everything."

"That sounds good to me."

We take separate cars, which is a little odd, considering we're going together, but it gives me a bit of time to collect myself.

As I wind along the familiar roads, I occasionally glance back in the rearview mirror, watching Vince talk on the phone as he follows me toward the diner I picked.

I'm slowly opening myself up to him, and it's partly because I realize I'm experiencing a totally different person than the one I've built up in my mind for so long. It's taken me a while to warm up to this understanding.

I think that's why Vince likes me—or at least wants to get to know me—because I don't treat him like everyone else does, putting him on a pedestal for show.

But it is a little ironic because, at this point, I'm the person who has benefitted from him the most.

It makes me wonder what he's getting out of the deal.

That thought stays on my mind as we sit in a hard plastic booth, and I watch him flip through the endless pages of brightly colored font and pictures of food until the waitress approaches to take our order.

Vince sticks with the classic burger and fries, quirking an eyebrow when I ask for the buffalo chicken salad with a side of pancakes.

"An odd combination," he says once we're alone.

"I feel like it's almost sacrilegious to come to a diner and not get breakfast food," I admit. "I'm not really a big salad person, but I don't think this one should even count. I mean, there are french fries and fried buffalo chicken bits on top. Bacon, too, and the entire thing is slathered in ranch."

It's the most I've ever spoken to him at once, and I'm rambling about a salad of all things.

Vince is unfazed by my sudden verboseness. "I'm

shocked, given how healthy your lunches are, that you would eat something like that," he teases.

I chuckle. "Blame Andy for the french fry mountain, not me. His parents are health nuts, so he likes to go overboard when he's not at home."

"My mom was like that for a while, too. She read every book on sports nutrition she could get her hands on, and it was especially terrible during my sophomore year when scouts started coming around."

"Wow, they waited until sophomore year?" I mock.

He chuckles. "Well, we can't all be Jake Montgomery."

I can feel my smile falter, and my reaction is reflected by the panic in his eyes.

"I'm sorry, I didn't—"

"Is Megan Rapinoe really your favorite player?" I ask him, scrambling for the first question I can think of that will immediately steer him away from the topic of my family.

He blinks, likely getting whiplash from my desperate subject change. "Yeah," he admits. "She is."

"Why?" I press.

"Because not only is she one of the best players in the world, she's unapologetic about who she is, especially in standing up for what's right. I admire the hell out of her."

"That's why she's *my* favorite," I tell him. "And because she has really cool hair."

"I've been thinking of trying that look out for myself," Vince grins, rubbing the back of his neck.

I shake my head, picturing how ridiculous he'd look with pink hair.

Actually, I take it back—if anyone has the confidence to pull something like that off, it's him.

"But my sisters would make fun of me endlessly," he adds.

"How many sisters do you have?" I ask.

And it's at this moment I consider that, despite the short amount of time I've actually spent with Vince—and the long period I've thought about him or known about his existence—I don't really know much about him.

It's one of those weird things, I think, where people are bystanders but think they are experts in someone else's life.

I can only begin to imagine what that experience has been like for him.

And how much worse it's going to get as he becomes a true star.

"Three," he says with a grimace. "Don't get me wrong, I love them all with everything I have, but I'm just the little brother they like to beat up on, even to this day."

Our food arrives, and as we eat, he tells me stories about the four of them growing up.

He got picked on relentlessly, apparently, and was forced to take part in their tea parties and be their guinea pig for trying out different shades of eyeshadow and lipstick.

I keep our conversation going with questions about him, wanting to dig deeper into his life and not give him much time to ask me about myself.

Even when he tries to volley the questions back to me, I give him superficial answers or little tidbits about funny moments with Andy, but I tiptoe around my family enough

I'm sure he picks up on the fact that it's not an area I'm ready to discuss with him.

Or anyone aside from Andy, really.

Despite Vince's earlier offer, I convince him to split the check with me, but I am a little sad our time is up.

And I'm at the point where I don't bother to fight or overanalyze my emotions.

Because I like Vince Novak.

That realization doesn't stun me at all because I think it's been true for a while, and I'm finally ready to admit it.

I glance over at him as he walks me to my car, and we're close enough that if I jutted my arm out, it would brush his.

For some reason, that makes me exceptionally nervous, but I try not to let it detract from appreciating these final few moments together.

"So, Andy gave me your number," Vince says, breaking the silence.

"Oh?"

He shoves his hands in his pockets. "Is that okay?"

"Yes."

"Good," he says with a smile.

"When did he give it to you?" I ask, curious.

"During lunch a few weeks ago," Vince admits. "I've been...I thought it'd be weird if I just texted you out of the blue."

"You know, you could have played it cool and just slyly asked me for it," I tease.

"I was under the assumption you and Andy told each other everything, though, and I didn't want to lie, even about something so trivial if it ever came up."

I appreciate his honesty here, but my thought from a few weeks ago floats to the forefront of my mind because I know he's lying to me about *something*...

He's not being entirely honest with me about the motive behind his move; however, since I'm unable to be forthcoming about my family life at the moment, it seems like a fair trade.

I think we're both content to live within these boundaries.

For now, at least.

"Thanks for inviting yourself," I say as I slide into my car. "I had a nice time."

"Me too. I guess I'll text you tomorrow?" His tone is hopeful, like he's sussing out my reaction.

"Okay," I return. "Tomorrow, then."

He offers me an easy grin, and my eyes, of course, are drawn to his mouth.

Only, this time, it's not just to look at that crooked tooth—it's to take in the shape of his lips and wonder what they would feel like on mine.

And that thought, so sudden and fleeting, is all I can think about as I drive home.

FOURTEEN

I spend most of Saturday holed up in my bedroom texting Vince.

We don't talk about anything in particular, but somehow, we manage to fill the entire day—minus the hour when he goes for a run—with a stream of messages back and forth.

I should be practicing my photography or touching up images in my portfolio, but I choose to sit on my bed by the window, either staring out at the downpour or checking my phone for whatever missives Vince sends me.

I'm giving myself permission to enjoy talking to him, and that alone feels like a gigantic step forward for me.

He gives me a little update about what he and his mom are up to—chores and watching television, mostly—but he also confesses to being a bit of a *Star Wars* fanatic.

After he gives me his definitive ranking of all the movies, I relent and give him small details about myself, but by my standards, there's really nothing interesting to report.

I frown at my realization that most of the stories I have to share are tied to Jake's random, short-lived passion projects or my following him around based on his schedule.

Really, given how much of a role soccer has played in both mine and Vince's lives, it's kind of impressive to fill an entire day's conversation without even one mention of it.

I'm curious if Vince notices, but I don't ask.

Instead, I confess I'm a little terrified of heights and how I once had an allergic reaction to poison ivy that was so bad I needed to be hospitalized for three days.

All of this culminates into what I discover might be my favorite part of texting—his sweet send-off as I fight to stay awake.

Sweet dreams, Maren.

For some reason, I find this message endearing, and I swear I drift off to sleep with a smile on my face.

I wake up exceptionally well rested and happy—both of which are a rarity for me these days.

It helps that the house is completely empty, and I have free rein in the kitchen.

As I slide two slices of bread into the toaster, I open my phone, wondering if it's my turn to start a texting conversation, since Vince did yesterday.

But given that it's bright and sunny outside, uncommon for this time of year in Pennsylvania, it's probably best that he spends the day outdoors training and I practice my photography.

As I bite into my toast, there's a knock at the front door.

Andy would just let himself in without hesitation, and we're definitely not expecting visitors at ten in the morning on a Sunday, so I ignore it at first, assuming it's a package, since my mom gets many delivered throughout the week.

When there's another knock, I sigh, drop my breakfast on a plate, and tiptoe over to the front window, breathing a sigh of relief when I peek through the curtains.

"Hey," I say after opening the door.

Uncle Eric grins and, without hesitation, pulls me into his arms.

The gesture surprises me, as does his presence at my house, but I soften into his chest immediately.

"Maren." His voice sounds more hoarse than I recall on non-game days.

We break our embrace, and I head toward the kitchen, offering him a cup of coffee from the pot my parents brewed before they left for church this morning.

Once it's heated in the microwave, I hand it over, and he accepts it gratefully.

"Everything okay?" I ask, which is my polite way of asking why he's here at all, let alone at this time of day.

He smiles, and I catch the glint in his eye. "I am so damn proud of you, you know that?"

"For what?" I ask, crunching down on the buttery brown crust.

He reaches behind his back and pulls the folded-up sports section of today's *Review* from his pocket.

With shaking hands, I unfold it and lay it flat on the

kitchen counter, smooth out the creases, then trace my own name in print.

I've submitted a few rounds of pictures to the paper, but only two have appeared online. I assume the majority are being put into some super special folder, ready to be used when Vince truly blows up into the star everyone says he's going to be.

Although print feels a little antiquated in some regards, according to Andy, anyway, given my recent adventures with the darkroom, I'm more inclined to appreciate tangible, physical art.

It feels permanent, in a way, to hold this in my hands.

"I'm going to buy a stack of these on the way home," he says, tapping the page. "But when I saw it this morning, I had to come over and congratulate you in person."

My fingertips move over Vince's jaw, captured by my own camera. His gaze is fixed in concentration right before he fires a penalty kick, which, of course, soared into the net.

I briefly take in the article itself, which is nothing much, really.

It's mostly just speculation about whether he will join the MLS club in Columbus or if he'll take Stanford up on their full-ride scholarship. There's even a brief quote from Uncle Eric, basically saying he has no comment on the matter and is focusing on his current team's championship season.

"Your parents around?" Uncle Eric asks.

I shake my head. "It's Sunday."

"Right," he breathes.

For as long as I've been aware, their weekend routine

has revolved around either sitting in bleachers or pews—neither of which I've been an active participant in since Jake died.

Which isn't saying much because other than photography and bothering Andy, I can't cop to being much of a participant in anything, really.

Except now I have Vince to text.

"You hungry?" I ask, waving to the bag of bread that's still sitting on the counter.

Uncle Eric smiles tightly at me. "I should get going, actually, before—"

"Maren?" My mother's voice is a little shrill as she enters through the front door. "Is someone here?"

Uncle Eric stiffens, standing up straight to greet her and my father.

As they cross into the kitchen, they both eye him like he's an intruder in their home instead of part of the family.

"What are you doing here?" It's my father who asks the question, and it's with a tone that's a mixture of disbelief and anger.

Uncle Eric gestures to me and the paper I didn't have time to hide.

"I came over to congratulate Maren in person for her very first published photo," he says proudly. "Front page of today's sports section."

Of course, he isn't exactly aware of my parents' disdain for my passion, but he's clued in immediately as their gazes flicker toward it and narrow.

It's not that impressive, I suppose, to have one measly picture printed, considering Jake's room is littered with stacks of newspapers about his career—all with hundreds of different photos that were *not* taken by me.

But to me, this means something.

No one moves or speaks in the aftermath of Uncle Eric's declaration, frozen in some standoff I don't wholly understand.

"Thank you for coming by, Uncle Eric," I say, finally mustering the courage to break the silence.

He blinks and refocuses on me, nodding slightly. "I meant what I said, Maren," he says before he lets himself out.

My parents don't move a muscle, watching me as I clean my plate and fold up the paper before bolting toward the safety of my room.

Before the door even closes, I hear the arguing start.

I grab my jacket and my film camera like it's my protection from the world and slip out of the house unnoticed. Starting my car would garner unwanted attention from my parents, so I resign myself to walking.

To where or for what purpose, I'm not sure.

With each step, I distance myself from the mess that is my family and simply try to embrace the world around me through a new lens.

I appreciate the neat rows of houses, the color of each turning leaf, the child who zooms by on a bike. It all seems so simple from my vantage point.

So why do we, as humans, make everything so damn complicated?

I don't have an answer for that question, but I do allow myself to get a little excited when my phone buzzes.

What are you up to? Vince asks.

Nothing much. Going for a walk and taking photos. You?

Just got cleaned up after my run.

I squeeze my eyes shut, holding onto the many mental pictures of how good he looks all sweaty and winded with the lines of his muscles defined from exertion.

He texts again. *Can I see you?*

My heart soars as I type up my response. *Can you pick me up?*

Yeah. Drop a pin.

It takes him less than twenty minutes to arrive.

When I slide in beside him, I'm practically suffocated—in the best way possible—by that combination of citrus, clove, and cinnamon.

"Hey," he says.

"Hi," I return, buckling in.

"Where do you want to shoot?"

"You sure you don't mind tagging along?" I ask him. "We can do something other than take photos."

He gives me a look like I'm out of my mind. "Are you kidding me? This is the best way to spend any Sunday."

I smile at him. "How about North Park?"

"My oldest sister, Ashley, used to take me there all the time," he recalls as he accelerates. "It was under the guise of giving my mom a break and taking me to get even more fresh air, but really, she used to meet up with her boyfriend while I went up and down the slide probably hundreds of times."

"Wow," I snort. "Have you ever confronted her for this injustice?"

Vince chuckles. "Well, I accidentally let it slip to my

mom what was happening, and I'm pretty sure Ashley got grounded for a month."

"Ouch."

"She probably got me back for it in some way," Vince admits.

I take a deep breath and volunteer one of my own stories.

"One time, when I was in middle school, Jake faked being sick to miss a weekend tournament, only to sneak out and go to a party with his girlfriend at the time. I fell asleep on the couch watching a movie and screamed bloody murder when he snuck in through the window, so the ruse was up."

It's the first time I can remember willingly sharing a story about my brother to anyone other than Andy, and it's oddly therapeutic.

Putting memories of him into the universe other than his soccer skills or his death is something I should be doing more of.

Because if I don't, who will?

This is a huge moment for me, but Vince breezes right by it, and I'm not sure if it's intentional.

"Rookie mistake on his part," he says lightly.

"Not letting me in on the plan?"

He shakes his head as he pulls us into an angled parking space. "Should have stayed out until morning," he declares as we exit the vehicle. "Sneaking back home in the middle of the night is dangerous, but if you wait until just before it's time to get up, you can act like you are casually getting breakfast or wanted to get an early start on the day."

I actually manage to laugh. "Are you saying that from experience?"

"Maybe," he says coyly as we walk along the path.

And suddenly, the same desire that crept up on Friday night to get to know him a little better becomes my most pressing need.

I want to understand every single thing about Vince Novak.

And not just the little things I picked up on yesterday, like his favorite color (blue) or his favorite food (quesadillas or lasagna, depending on the day), but real things. Like his deepest fears, the ones buried so deep he's afraid to unpack them, and if his heart has ever been so shattered that it throbs with every single beat.

I'm wracking my brain for a way to even broach the subject without coming off as insane, but Vince speaks first.

"You ever been kayaking?" he asks curiously, like he's gauging my interest to see if that's something we can do together.

He tilts his head toward a small group of people laughing and struggling to navigate their kayaks as they slowly float across the water in front of us.

Admittedly, it would probably be a refreshing way to see the park, giving me a new vantage point to take photos, but I swallow in dread.

It's so smooth on the surface, somehow glassy yet rippled, but it's deadly beneath.

I, of all people, know this to be true.

It was easy enough when I confessed my fear of heights to Vince to back it up with horror stories.

But there's one thing I'm even more terrified of that I don't dare speak about in fear that people will ask questions.

Water.

One glance at Jake Montgomery's obituary—the first result that pops up when searching his name—is explanation enough.

"Maren?" Vince asks.

"Sorry," I say quietly. "I left for a second."

He nods, eyes raking over my features, and lets the subject of kayaking drop. "So, what do you do when you come here to take photos?"

"I just kind of wander around until inspiration strikes," I admit. "It's not that great of a process, but I think sometimes I need to ease into it, appreciate the beauty before I can even begin to document it."

"I like that," Vince says.

We walk side by side, away from the water and up a jogging trail, and I hold the camera up to my eye, seeing if there's anything worth capturing.

Vince is content to indulge this practice, awarding me endless patience as I randomly stop but don't ultimately spare my film on what I see.

That is, until the path curves, and I let out an excited breath.

"Here," I say, leading him off the path and into a little grassy area.

Vince follows without hesitation.

I'm pleased that although we're completely shrouded in beautiful orange and yellow hues of fall leaves, the sun peeks through.

I lower to my knees, then sink down completely to get just the right angle of colors, sunshine, and Vince.

"Can I join you?" he asks, unaware that I'm trying to make him the subject of my photo. "Or will that disrupt the creative process?"

"The grass is a little wet from yesterday," I warn him.

He shrugs and joins me, trying to see from my point of view.

I prop myself up on my elbow as I glance around, and Vince turns his head toward me while the rest of him stays sprawled on the grass.

He appears thoroughly content to watch me work through this, like he doesn't have a care in the world or some bright future ahead of him—he's just here, in the moment with me, enjoying the experience.

I wish I could be that carefree.

"Do you mind if I take a few pictures of you?" I ask him.

Vince shakes his head. "Should I pose?"

"No," I say quickly. "Do whatever is comfortable."

I lean forward, homing in on him.

In the awkwardness of having a lens so close to his face, he smiles, and I get that perfect little flaw, contrasted so beautifully by his skin and our surroundings.

I fire off a few pictures, almost wishing I had my digital camera so I could see the results immediately, but I adjust the angle and click some more, smiling at him when I finally lower the camera.

"Do you ever take pictures of yourself?" Vince asks, running his fingers through the fallen leaves.

I laugh. "No."

"Well, can you teach me?"

"Sure," I say, biting down on the corner of my lip. "Although, it's pretty easy. Since I have all the settings in place, you just have to click the button."

He shakes his head. "No, I want to understand what makes something worthy of being captured by Maren Montgomery, not just the mechanics of taking a photo."

And so I tell him.

I spill it all, mostly incoherently and a little shyly, but I tell him what I look for, how my eye is drawn to the unique, imperfect parts of being human or existing in the world.

"I think I've got it," Vince says quietly, holding out his hand for the camera.

The act of handing it over, and trusting him with it, is like giving him a piece of my soul.

"Thank you," he says seriously, as if he understands the responsibility. "Lie back, please."

Unlike my lack of direction when photographing him, he asks me to spread my hair beneath me and let my arms fall back, like I'm opening myself up.

It feels odd, but not entirely unpleasant, to surrender to the world around me.

He stands, blocking out the sun in the sky, and I meet his gaze, challenging him to pick out the perfect shot based on my own logic.

The sound of the shutter releasing from this side of the camera makes me gasp slightly.

And then this moment between us is officially solidified into permanence.

"What is my little flaw?" I ask lightly as he reaches out to help me up.

When our skin touches, I swear it's electric and magical and so many things all at once.

Vince returns my camera once I've brushed myself off. "You'll see when you develop the film."

"Okay," I say. "Now, let's go get some free ice cream from Andy."

He extends his hand toward me again, and I stare at it for at least three heartbeats before I slide my fingers into his.

We walk together, appreciating our surroundings and the tangible link between us as we make our way toward Dream Freeze.

I can't even begin to imagine what flavor Andy is going to give me when he sees Vince and me together.

FIFTEEN

It's so subtle, I don't even notice it at first, but as the days continue, Vince Novak works his way further into my daily life.

I've already spent more time than I should thinking about him, but now, those thoughts are trumped by action. Instead of recalling the lines of his cheekbones or how surprisingly muscular his arms are for a center forward, I photograph him at practice, text him at night, and let him walk me to classes.

In fact, things progress so naturally that I don't even question it when he sits next to me, thigh flush against mine in the tiny seat on the bus that's taking us downtown for a history field trip.

We pass the time stuck in traffic by playing some pixelated soccer game on his phone, getting more competitive each time one of us outscores the other, and blocking out the chatter around us.

In the museum itself, we walk side by side as our

teacher and the museum guide lead us through the exhibit on American democracy—which specifically relates to the unit we're working through—then after that, we're given free rein.

Vince poses in front of the eleven-foot ketchup bottle as I snap photos on my phone, then we mill around, looking at artifacts from the 1800s and reading the placards that go deeper into detailing the displays.

At least, I'm *pretending* to be enthralled with the history around me, but really, I'm so conscious of the way Vince's knuckles graze mine ever so slightly when we walk and the scent of oranges invading my senses as he leans in, saying he needs to get a closer look.

I've seen him drill a shot into the net from midfield without so much as a squint, so I know for certain he doesn't *have* to rest his chin on my shoulder, but I don't call him out on it.

I'm too busy trying not to squirm in excitement.

"It should be a light practice today," Vince says as we linger in front of a set of vintage advertisements.

"Right, you have that away game against Central tomorrow," I murmur, knowing that Uncle Eric doesn't run his players too hard before big games in favor of doubling down on strategy and stretching.

Vince shoves his hands in his pockets. "I was wondering if you'd want to come over after."

"Over?" I clarify. "Like, to your house?"

He smiles. "It's an apartment, but yes."

"And do what?" I ask tentatively.

My hesitation causes him to chuckle.

"Do you always have to have an agenda to spend time with someone?" Vince questions.

"No," I respond.

But I'm lying.

The first and last time I did something without a purpose was going to the party with Andy, but even then, I was fueled by my own selfish desire to prove Andy and myself wrong.

I chew on my lip. "But...what would we do?"

"Watch TV, do homework, eat?" Vince suggests. "Whatever people do when they hang out."

"Right," I say.

It's so normal when he says it like that, but being alone with a guy who smells this good and is expressing interest in me...

This is uncharted territory.

I glance around to see for once, thankfully, everyone is too preoccupied with other things to be paying attention to Vince.

"Have you had a lot of girlfriends?" I ask him.

It's a subject we have yet to broach—mostly because I hoped he would never bring it up. But I haven't forgotten about that speculation of his past girlfriend the day I found out he was transferring to Greene.

Vince, for the first time I've ever seen, looks taken aback by my question. "Uh, I mean, I've dated a few girls."

"When was your last relationship?"

"We broke up over the summer."

I nod, slightly relieved he says this without a shred of pain, signaling he's very much over it. "Why?"

"It's...complicated," he says with a frown. "She's a great

person who didn't want to do long distance. But, really, it comes down to that we just didn't work out, and I'm fine with it."

"Okay."

"And what about you?" Vince asks.

I knew this question would come when I opened the floodgate, but I'm actually happy to clear the air and put the truth out there, just so he understands I might not have the same level of expertise on this subject.

"Never," I admit quietly.

"Hopefully, we can change that," he says, sliding his hand into mine.

I swallow as I meet his gaze, wondering if he can feel how my hand shakes just a little bit in his.

"Come on," he says, leading me toward the next exhibit. "Let's see if there's anything else worth posing in front of in this place."

For the rest of the day, Vince and I are in our own little bubble.

It's like the simple gesture of our hands being intertwined sends a signal to everyone around us to leave us alone, serves as a barrier against those who would usually approach him without question.

On the bus ride home, I'm more comfortable around him, deliberately leaning into him as we both look out the window, watching the city zoom by as we head back toward the school.

We reluctantly part ways until he's finished with practice, and then I head to the address he messaged me, trying to dampen my nerves along the way.

I finally gather my resolve as I knock on his front door.

Only, it's not Vince who greets me but his mother.

"Oh," I say.

It's not the best first impression I could hope to make on someone.

"You must be Maren," she says, offering me a genuine smile.

I nod. "It's nice to meet you, Mrs. Novak."

She scrunches her nose. "You can come in only if you drop the title. My mother-in-law was Mrs. Novak, and I am *definitely* nothing like her." She laughs at the idea. "'Tiffany' is fine."

"Okay." I give her what I think is a nervous grin.

She waves me inside. "Watch out for the boxes," she warns.

I blink and nearly stumble into a set of stacked cardboard moving boxes.

There are at least two dozen of them lined up along the wall like some sort of barrier, completely crowding the living room space.

"I don't even know what's in these," she admits. "Some of the boxes are from my mom's house, some are from my uncle's, and some...I can't even begin to guess. I've been so busy that I haven't had a chance to sort everything out since they both packed up and headed for warmer weather in Florida. And now, since we'll only be here through the school year, it doesn't really make much sense to go through them."

"Right," I say. "So, you're going to move wherever Vince goes?"

"We'll see," she answers.

I nod, understanding she doesn't want to give anything away.

"For instance," she continues, "if he accepts one of the scholarships, I think I'll take a pass on reliving my college years. But, if he accepts a lucrative deal from one of the Italian teams, let's just say I am more than fine with going off my no-carb diet."

"And you don't have any preference?" I can't help but ask.

"Oh, I definitely do," she says with a snort.

I run my hand along the sides of the boxes, trying to suppress the urge to open them as I follow her toward the kitchen, and wonder what treasures are buried within.

"I just watched a show where this woman cleaned out her attic and found a set of dishware that was worth thirty thousand dollars," I tell her.

She laughs. "I'm definitely not holding out for that, but I like where your head's at. It's probably just my uncle's collection of baseball caps and every Christmas card my mother ever received."

I'm unfamiliar with the notion of such keepsakes because aside from Jake's shrine-slash-bedroom, my parents very clearly aren't sentimental.

There aren't a lot of pictures of us, or throw pillows, or knickknacks from my childhood, and even though we've lived in the same house my entire life, somehow this two-bedroom apartment—even being half packed-up—seems more lived in and loved than what I experience at home.

"Hey," Vince says, stepping into the kitchen. "I didn't realize you were here yet."

"I am."

I shift on my feet, unsure how I'm supposed to properly greet him or if I'm supposed to do so at all because it's only been an hour since we last saw each other, and his mom is here...

"Mom, we're going to do homework in my room," he says, grabbing my hand and leading me away before I can overthink the display of affection.

"Door open, though," she calls.

"Yeah, yeah."

We sit down on the floor, side by side, with our backs against his bedframe, and, to my surprise, we actually do homework.

Vince uses one of the moving boxes in the room as a desk, and we knock out our history assignment—a recap of our field trip today—two days early before continuing on to our other subjects.

I'm about halfway through a really frustrating math problem when Vince scoots closer to me, eliminating the very defined gap of space between us.

"I'm done doing homework," he announces.

"I'm not," I tell him, pretending to go back to my work.

He laughs and leans his head back.

I force myself to keep my attention fixed on this seemingly impossible problem, though my concentration further dwindles as Vince's hand slowly ticks up from the floor and onto my jean-clad thigh.

I press my lips together as his pinky finger moves in little figure eights, somehow searing my skin through the material.

My face flushes as I squirm, and he smiles in victory at successfully distracting me.

I shove my school stuff back in my bag, then angle myself toward him, curious as to what he's going to do next.

He brushes my hair back behind my shoulder, giving him an unobstructed view of my face.

That one little gesture, like pushing back a shield, makes me feel exposed and nervous and exhilarated.

I lick my lips as my heart pounds, hoping like hell this is leading where I think it's about to.

"I know you've been through a lot, Maren," he says lowly. "With Jake—"

I frown and drop my gaze to my hands, wringing them together.

Vince tilts my chin up, locking his eyes on mine. "I think it's going to take some time for you to feel comfortable opening up."

I nod. "Yeah."

"But you should know that I am."

"What?"

"Ready. To hear whatever is on your mind whenever you are."

I know he means it.

And acknowledging that truth is somewhat terrifying.

"You didn't like me when we first met, and sometimes I think you still don't," he teases. "You're not like anyone else, and I know part of that is because of who you are, what you've been through, and who I am, but I'll take whatever you can give me. Hell, I've never been so content to be taken off guard or be stared at through the lens of a camera before I met you."

A smile tugs at the edge of my lips.

"And I don't need you to make any promises or big declarations," he presses. "I just need to know...do you think you could eventually be content with me, too?"

My breathing picks up as I consider the weight of that question, and my eyes land on my own photo—the framed one of the dead bird—hanging up on the wall of his bedroom.

"You kids hungry?" Vince's mom calls from the hall, breaking us from our trance.

"Yes," I say aloud, answering both questions at once.

SIXTEEN

I don't have a flavor of ice cream for happy.

The realization hits me as I reorganize the makeshift darkroom, taking notes of what supplies I need to stock up on to develop the photos from last weekend.

My mind wanders to Vince, as it usually does, and then to thinking about how I should finish up to go see Andy at work…

And I don't have a flavor of ice cream for happy.

In my many moods that Andy has documented, this one hasn't been present enough to justify its own trademark. Out of all the pain and depressing thoughts I've had to overcome in the past few years, this somehow guts me in a way I haven't experienced.

Before Jake died, I was a normal, bubbly teenager.

I played soccer when I wasn't cheering my brother on, had sleepovers and Friday night outings with Andy, and concerned myself with all the frivolously wonderful things about life that I've shied away from ever since.

Jake was the happiest person I've ever known, the life of every single party and situation, the one who made me laugh endlessly with impressions of cartoon characters.

I can't even remember the last time I laughed like that.

Some days, my smile still feels a little foreign to me, like I'm attempting to revive atrophied muscles.

With shaking hands, I gather up my belongings and drive home, needing to get as far away from these thoughts as I can, but they grow exponentially in my solitude.

This is exactly why Andy's three most notable moods assigned to me are pensive, angry, and caught up in too many emotions to count.

Right now, I'm all of them all at once.

Music doesn't do its job of distracting me in the car, so when I arrive home, I drop my bag on the table and dash up the stairs toward my room so I can break down completely or do whatever feels right at the moment.

As I trace my hand over Jake's door on my way past, like I always do, something makes me stop.

It's been years since I've cracked open this door, and back then, I was a different person. Now, I don't know who I am or what I'm doing, but my heart pounds in my ears, propelling me forward as I slowly turn the knob.

I step in with no expectation of how I'll feel or what I'll do, but I become completely numb as my eyes take in the room.

It's a physical portrait of the life Jake once lived.

There's a thin layer of dust across the obscene number of trophies on the shelf, and his desk is just as he left it. The surface is scattered with pen caps and random notecards from the tests he was studying for over his last Thanksgiving break at home.

I slide open the closet to run my fingers over the logo shirts and button-downs that are in desperate need of ironing and take in the massive pile of cleats. Some still have mud and grass caked on them.

Jake would hate this.

Not just this room but my reaction to it—how I've become a shell of the person I once was, dragged down by my own sadness and the broken relationships in our family.

I sink to the floor and lean against his bedframe.

It's an odd parallel to sit here with the ghost of my brother and myself, when with Vince, in a similar position in his room, I've never felt more alive.

The tears roll down my cheeks, and I don't bother wiping them away.

It's actually kind of refreshing to let myself cry and feel grief and sorrow so wholly, so I double down, letting the sob overtake my body just because I can.

I quickly become addicted to the release, not the tears or the sadness, necessarily, but letting myself go.

I reach my hands behind me and claw at the comforter, coughing as the fabric falls around me and dust disperses through the room, then rush to crack the window.

After years of not being used, it has to be heaved from the sill, and when I finally succeed in mustering all my strength, the cold air whooshes through the room.

Every piece of errant paper—little scribbles and notes marred by Jake's handwriting—soars through the air like it's as free as I feel at this moment.

"Maren, what the *hell* are you doing?!" my dad yells as he appears in the doorway.

I don't have words to explain the rush of emotions, so I stand silently with my chest rapidly rising and falling as my dad stomps across the room to slam the window shut.

He scrambles to pick up the papers, putting them back just as Jake left them.

"Your mother's going to go ballistic when she sees this," he seethes. "Pick up the comforter."

"No," I say automatically.

I can't decide if this is my breaking point or the exact moment my backbone has decided to regrow, but I'm going with it.

His jaw clenches in irritation, face turning red at my defiance. "What did you say?"

"Jake wouldn't want us to do this." I gesture around the room. "Not just this room but how we are living without him."

"You don't know that," my father snaps. "You don't know what it's like."

Part of me wants to cling to the anger bubbling up inside me and fire off at him like my mom does, but I rise above it.

"I do know," I say calmly, which only infuriates him more. "And I'm not going to live like this anymore."

I brush past him and bound down the steps.

I've said my piece, and I'm not going to stick around to deal with my mother or to hash this out with him further.

But, of course, she arrives home just as my feet hit the landing, and her murderous expression freezes me in place.

"What is this?" she demands.

I expect her to go nuclear over the disturbance of Jake's bedroom, but her rage is actually directed at the large envelope in her hands.

It's addressed to me, but she, apparently, took the liberty of opening it.

The proof copy of the collaboration calendar is gripped between her fingers so tightly that there are nail marks embedded in the cover photo.

"It's nothing," I say, reaching for it.

She pulls it just out of my grasp before I can make contact.

"Maren," my father's voice booms.

I turn to see his eyes fall on my mother's tight expression.

"Kerri, I'll have the room put back together in a minute," he says quickly.

"What?" Her gaze flickers up the stairs to see Jake's door ajar before her eyes narrow at me. "What did you do, Maren?"

"She trashed it," my father answers for me.

My mouth drops open. "I didn't—"

"And then mouthed off to me about it," he steamrolls over me.

As strange as it is to see them on the same side for once, it's not lost on me that the only common ground they've found since Jake died is the ability to gang up on me and chide me for not going along with exactly what they've planned.

I'm sick of it.

But on some level, I also feel bad for them.

Pity is not an emotion I appreciate when directed

toward me, but it's one they've long accepted from other people.

This is the first time they've gotten it from their own daughter.

Grief is an awful, weighty thing, and I've always tried to understand what they're going through. Adults are supposed to have everything figured out—or at least be able to help their kids find some direction—but I think when Jake died, part of them fractured and never healed.

So I'm stuck dealing with the fallout.

However, I've got enough to deal with on my own without trying to save my parents from their constant misery, so I grab my bag and try to get back outside.

But my attempt to slip past my mother doesn't go as planned, as she grabs the strap on my backpack and yanks it backward.

I'm able to stop myself from tumbling, and I take a beat to steady myself before surging ahead, desperate to run to my car and lock myself in.

However, as I move forward, my mother lets go of my backpack, and the loss of the grip causes it to hit the floor with a sickening *thud*.

The sound of my camera smashing against the tile is dampened slightly by the fabric of my bag, but I surely hear the unmistakable sound of something snapping.

I give up on my quest to escape, immediately falling to my knees and scrambling to see the damage.

It's always easy to say what should have or could have been done to prevent whatever bad thing has happened, like how I should have coughed up the money for a reinforced, padded case for the camera.

But that doesn't matter now because I have to deal with the reality of being devastated by the sight of the old, fragile camera cracked and bent.

"You're grounded," my father barks as my mother steps in front of the door again, boxing me in.

Tears blur my vision at this entire frustrating situation.

I hold the broken camera to my chest and grab my backpack from the floor, along with the calendar—which she now gives up easily—and stomp upstairs to my room.

I flip the lock on the door, collapse on my bed, curled up around the broken camera, and let myself cry.

It's barely been an hour since I hightailed it out of school, and I've been on a dangerous rollercoaster of emotions since.

It hurts to feel everything.

But it's also good because, to allow myself to open up and enjoy my life, I'm going to have to work through it all.

I think back to a conversation I had weeks ago with Michael, of all people, during one of Andy's shifts at Dream Freeze.

"So, you really don't want to take over the family business?" I ask him, recalling our conversation in the cafeteria about his desire to break out on his own.

Michael glances around, like his father might be listening. "I don't, but it's not exactly public knowledge."

"Right," I cringe. "Sorry."

He sighs. "It's just another secret I have to keep."

"But everything's going to come out eventually, right?" I ask, watching my best friend as he chats with a little ballerina about what flavor of dip she wants.

Michael smiles at the sight. "I hope so. But hope can only get you so far."

"So what are you going to do about it?" I ask him curiously.

He glances over at me, so nonchalant but somehow homing in on something buried deep inside me. "What are you going to do about it?"

I shrugged him off then, but I have an answer now—finally, all this time after Jake's death, I'm ready to take back my life.

With shaking hands, I dig out my photography books from under my bed and rifle through the pages until my fingers find Abigail Archer's business card.

It's been embarrassingly long since Mr. Wilde offered me this lifeline, but I don't let that stop me.

I type out an email, introducing myself to her and thanking her for letting Mr. Wilde pass along her card, saying if the offer still stands, I would love to come by and see her gallery someday.

Before I hit send, I second-guess myself about being too open-ended, but I also don't want to come across as too aggressive or needy, since she's doing me a kindness. Deciding to leave it as is, I squeeze my eyes shut and hit the button.

Within ten minutes, but after a bit of pacing on my part, I get a reply.

Maren,

Great to finally hear from you.

I'm currently out of town, visiting my son and his fiancée in New

York, and when I return, I'm afraid my calendar is very full in preparation for launching a new showing at the gallery.

But I would love for you to attend the opening. Will have my assistant provide the details. Then we can plan a day and time to review your portfolio.

Talk soon,

Abigail

I read the message five times before I finally smile.

SEVENTEEN

The door to the art room creaks when Mr. Wilde steps inside. "Maren."

I roll my shoulders back, trying to eradicate any lingering tension from my hunched position, but I keep my eyes on my computer. "Thanks for meeting me early," I say as I cue up the photos.

"Of course," he dismisses. "Anything for my favorite student."

I beam at that but keep my gaze focused on organizing my folder just how I want it.

He sits down beside me, smelling of coffee and cologne, and leans in.

"Here," I offer, turning the laptop toward him so he can flip through my pictures at his own pace.

Mr. Wilde smiles at me fully before he dives into the little worlds I've captured.

I don't watch the screen as he slowly makes his way through the batch of images...

I look at him.

And not one miniscule head tilt or nod goes unnoticed by my scrutiny.

I'm dying to get his commentary and hear every single little thought going through his mind, but I don't ask. I just sit back, wait, and chew on my bottom lip.

Finally, after a full ten minutes of silence, he speaks.

"What were you thinking when you took this?" He's stopped on one of the many pictures I took over the summer outside Dream Freeze, zoomed in on some of the chipped paint from the newly installed WE'RE OPEN! sign.

I can't pinpoint exactly what day that was or what mood I was even in.

"I don't remember," I admit softly.

He nods, expression tight. "It shows."

I flinch.

"Why don't you have any of your print photos on here?" he asks, sitting back. "They're some of your strongest pieces."

"You think so?"

"These are good," he says evenly, then pauses, letting the words hit me as he runs his fingers through his hair. "But those pictures you displayed at the fundraiser...those were great. Even without knowing the work you put into developing, I could sense a level of involvement in the process that I hadn't seen from you yet."

It's interesting he says that, considering those photos were actually meant to be throwaways.

There's something to be learned from it, I suppose.

Like if I let go of trying to reach for perfection, I actually get closer to it.

"If you don't mind looking again, I'll see what I can capture after practice tonight and this weekend," I tell him.

He bites the edge of his lip. "About that..."

"Is something wrong?" I ask, slipping my computer into my backpack.

"I debated saying anything, but the truth is, Maren...I would hate for you to get distracted at such a crucial time."

I blink rapidly. "I'm not sure what you mean."

"This soccer player," he continues. "He seems to be taking up a lot of your time."

"Some of my free time, yes, but mostly, I'm taking pictures for the *Gazette* to—"

"Do you want to be a photojournalist?"

"I don't know."

"Because if so, great—take those stills of sweaty teenagers running around, and get a grainy photo." He stops, hardening his gaze. "But if you want to be a *real* photographer, Maren, a master of an art, it's going to require everything you've got."

I swallow, digesting his words.

"He's a distraction," he insists.

Suddenly, I feel strange about baring my personal work to this man, trusting his opinions so wholly when he can't even see the slight but positive change in me recently.

Then again, he doesn't really know anything about me, does he?

He's my teacher, and for as much as I've considered him a friend, he's in no real position to make these statements.

"Aren't you the one who said you do your best painting after lovemaking?" I counter, recalling the words he let spill out during a critique session last spring.

He blinks like I've slapped him, and I grimace, immediately regretting my words.

"I'm sorry," I tell him.

He stands up and crosses the room, like he has to physically back away from this conversation.

"That was inappropriate of me to say," I admit.

Mr. Wilde doesn't respond, but I see him gripping the edge of a stool—the same one I sit at in front of the window every day—so hard his knuckles turn white.

"I'll, uh, see you in class later," I mumble as I practically sprint from the room.

It takes me a full five minutes of fast walking through the hallways to shake loose the rock in my stomach.

I promised myself I would start feeling and speaking and *living*, but maybe I shouldn't let my annoyance bubble up quite so easily.

My dedication to stepping out of my comfort zone is so new that I need to reacquaint myself with how to rein and flex my reactions when it's appropriate.

I'm like a live wire, sparking wildly and ready to catch something on fire, but truthfully, I don't mind it.

The pressure inside me lessens as I continue throughout the day to not actively hide myself and my emotions from the world.

And no one seems more pleased at this than Andy.

"Who are you?" he asks with a smirk, dragging his eyes up and down my exterior as I join him at lunch.

To the untrained eye, I look the same as I do every day, but Andy picks up on the subtle changes: I took extra care in straightening my hair this morning, wore one of my newer shirts that he says complements the color of my eyes, and most importantly, I dug out my confidence from somewhere deep in the dregs of my closet.

When Vince sits beside me at the table, I make the first move to slide up against him, slipping my hand in his while he picks at his plate with the other.

Andy's eyes practically bug out of his head as he frantically texts me, *You're holding out on me, Maren Montgomery!!!!*

I'm actually surprised he's containing himself enough to *send* those words to me instead of bursting them out loud.

Am not! I respond.

You are literally HOLDING Vince Novak's hand two feet away from me. Where there are PEOPLE around. This isn't DREAM FREEZE!!! THIS IS REAL LIFE!!!

Michael and Vince carry on a conversation about some television show they both watch while I stretch my thumb to respond to Andy.

I roll my eyes. *It's all real life.*

YOU ARE FIXATING ON THE WRONG PART OF THIS, MAREN. I NEED DETAILS. WHAT HAS HAPPENED THAT I DO NOT KNOW ABOUT.

Nothing much. Holding hands is pretty much the extent of it.

Really?

Really.

Come by Dream Freeze after practice. I think it's a vanilla day.

I bite back a grin. *I think we need a new flavor.*

After I hit send, I meet Andy's eyes, watching how he takes in the comfort between Vince and me.

He presses his lips together to hide his smile while shaking his head, as if he's some sort of proud parent—not that I know what that's like.

Something with a cherry on top, Andy texts back, then shoves his phone in his pocket.

"What do you think, Maren?" Vince asks, pulling me into the flow of the conversation. "Is Michael's obsession with *The Office* justified?"

Andy rolls his eyes and answers on my behalf. "Definitely not."

I chuckle, listening to the two of them argue until the bell rings for our next class.

Despite the heaviness of yesterday, and how off-putting Mr. Wilde's warning was this morning, I enjoy the rest of the day.

I ignore Mr. Wilde in art class and help a junior string up a canvas, and I even voluntarily raise my hand to answer a question in history, which surprises Vince.

At practice, with my trusted and unbroken digital camera in my hands, I decide to stop taking what photos I think people will like or what's trendy and just trust my eye.

The pieces currently in my portfolio are mostly abstract, and although I like to seek out the perfect little flaws in my environment, I try to take a step back now and really capture the *feeling* of the frame, not just what I'm trying to pull from it.

It's pretty challenging, given most of my targets are moving.

As the players run through sets of drills, I walk around, trying out different vantage points to see if that jars anything, but it's not until Vince lines up near the goal that inspiration strikes.

I move toward the back of the net and wave to him.

He adjusts the ball to precisely where he wants it, then idles until I get in position and hold my hand up above the camera, signaling for him to angle the ball just so.

I snap a few shots as he takes a deep breath, righting himself before he sends it directly at the intended target of my palm.

The photos I take are cool, but I don't know if they're portfolio worthy.

Vince jogs over and gushes—but he seems to like all of my photos, no matter the subject or medium—then Uncle Eric yells at him to get his ass back to practice.

I hover around for the rest of the drills, and after the team's quick wrap-up meeting, everyone disperses.

It's my cue to leave, but as I start toward the parking lot, intending to head anywhere but home, Vince puts a hand on my hip, tugging me back toward the field.

"Come on," he dribbles a ball over toward the center circle. "I've been thinking about what you said the other night in my room."

I run my fingers through the ends of my hair. "Which part?"

"You and I both carry things we're not ready to share with the world."

"I've been thinking about that a lot, actually," I admit.

He nods. "Me too. Which is why I was thinking...maybe if I share something with you, you'll share with me?"

My lips part in surprise. "You want to trade secrets?"

"I want to do so much more than that with you, Maren," he answers seriously. "But this is a start."

"Okay," I breathe.

He quirks an eyebrow. "I thought I was going to have to

do a lot more to get you to agree. I had a little speech prepared and everything."

I chuckle. "I'd still like to hear the speech."

"No way," Vince scoffs. "I'll save it for the next round."

He glances around, ensuring we're alone before he steps closer to me. "I want to tell you the real reason I transferred to Greene."

I suck in a breath, waiting for some nefarious truth to surface.

But somehow, what he tells me is worse than I imagined.

"My sister, Mary, the one that's only two years older than me, dated my coach," he tells me slowly. "I didn't even know what was happening until they broke up." He sighs and digs his cleats into the soft grass. "Obviously, it didn't end well, and after overhearing my sister sob to my mom about some of the...less than appealing details, I was done."

He pauses to collect himself, and I see each wisp of his exhales in the air as they leave his mouth.

"I didn't learn until last August that she was only seventeen when they started dating. He's...a lot older and very married," Vince explains with a grimace.

The pit in my stomach grows, deepening with each passing second.

"She's really embarrassed about the entire thing, but even worse..." His voice breaks slightly, and I reach for his hand. "Her main concern was over *my* career if the news ever came out."

He shakes his head, trying to rid himself of the emotion.

"I'll be damned if something I'm in control of hurts someone I love. So it was the simplest thing to transfer and spew that bullshit about only caring about winning. Don't get me wrong, a championship would be great, but doing my part to lessen my sister's pain and mortification was my real priority."

I'm a little embarrassed that I was so irritated by the thought of him and his ego when he might just be the kindest, sweetest, most wonderful person I've ever met.

And he, with all that goodness, wants to spend time with me.

Everyone wants a piece of Vince Novak for the glory of who he is going to become, but truly, it's an honor to get to know who he is right now at this exact moment.

"Besides," he continues, forcing a light tone. "I don't think I could even bring myself to look at my coach without punching him in the face."

Despite the gravity, we both laugh.

"And now, that brings me to you."

I bite my lip, trying to decide what secret I'll trade with him.

"I want to see you," he says, nodding to the ball on the ground.

Compared to what he just confessed, it's laughable, really, how simple it would be to move my leg and send the ball soaring across the field.

But that doesn't make the action, or the history behind it, easier.

He takes a step back, sensing I need a minute to prepare.

I close my eyes, imagining, instead of being here in this

field where I've watched Jake thrive so spectacularly, I'm back in simpler times, in our backyard, kicking a ball back and forth just because we wanted to pass the time together.

When I can almost hear the sound of my brother's laughter and smell the scent of oranges on my fingertips, I finally meet Vince's gaze.

He immediately takes off, calling for a pass downfield.

I kick my right leg forward, testing the motion before I start to dribble.

I move slowly at first, then soon enough, all the tension leaves my body, like it hasn't been years since I've done this.

Each step forward feels like I'm walking into the safety of a home that I thought didn't exist for me anymore.

I pick up my pace, exhilarated by the movement, and easily pass the ball up to Vince, whose feet have just stepped inside the penalty area.

It'd be an easy shot for him to take—too easy, actually—but he immediately sends it back to me.

Though I'm on the run, it's queued up perfectly for me to launch it, so I do.

The ball soars into the back of the net.

Vince pumps his arms in the air and yells in excitement, like I've just won some major tournament, and I match his enthusiasm, letting my grin slice my face in half.

He wraps his arms around my waist and lifts me up in celebration, spinning me around.

I laugh as he lowers me back to the ground and refuses to relinquish his hold on me.

Over his shoulder, a car's headlights turn on, but it's

not until the driver has backed out of his space completely that I see it's Uncle Eric.

And I think it's fitting he got to witness this moment.

"Let's do that again," Vince suggests. "I'll stand in the goal, and you can *try* to get some shots past these hands."

"You're on," I say, then make quick work of lining it up just how I want it.

Vince positions himself in the middle of the net, bouncing on his toes with the most serious look I've ever seen on his face, waiting to decide if he should dive left or right.

"If you miss this, you owe me another secret," he calls.

I can do better than that.

"Okay," I return, then channel my exhilaration into boldness. "But if I make it, there's something I want in return."

"What?"

"If I make it, we're going on a *real* date. Not to a diner or wandering around a park. I'm talking dinner and a movie and all that contentedness you talked about wanting to have with me."

He smiles. "Done."

As I move, Vince quits his bouncing and stands rigidly in place, letting me chip the ball in easily.

I've never seen a goalie so happy to be scored on.

EIGHTEEN

When my father grounded me for my "bad behavior," he gave me no rules or timeframe.

I've never actually been grounded before, so I think he just defaulted to the typical parental response for such a heated moment.

Honestly, I'm surprised he had it in him.

However, since temper spikes and arguments occur regularly in our home without any consequences, I'm simply going to pretend my punishment doesn't exist.

That shouldn't be too hard.

After all, I've perfected invisibility since Jake died, and my parents have enabled this by being so absent, so I'm used to slipping into rooms and out of the house unnoticed.

I change into another dress I've never worn, layer it over a pair of black tights, step into my highest heeled boots, and finally, swipe on a layer of the lipstick Andy *conveniently* left in my bathroom the other day.

I bound out of the house when Vince pulls up.

He gets out of the car to greet me like a gentleman, but I bypass the formalities entirely, waving him off and buckling in quickly, eager to get away from my house and on with our first official date.

"You okay?" Vince asks, picking up on my fidgeting. "Excited?"

"Yes to both," I say, finally breathing as we turn out of my neighborhood.

It's Halloween, and the trick-or-treaters are already running up and down the sidewalks in droves.

I remember what it was like to be that age, carefree while running around with Andy in search of our next sugar fix.

"What was your best Halloween costume?" I ask.

Vince laughs and taps on the steering wheel. "One year, my sisters went as the Ghostbusters. One guess as to who the ghost was."

I snort. "I'm definitely going to need to see pictures."

"A box in my room is filled with photo albums, so I can probably find one," Vince says. "My uncle's favorite hobby was apparently documenting all of my games and whatever antics my sisters put me through. What was your favorite costume?"

I consider it. "One year, Andy and I went as Mario and Luigi, which was definitely our most elaborate costume, but my favorite was when we went as a peanut butter and jelly sandwich. It was so easy to make but really hard to move around in."

"Who was the jelly?"

"Andy. But only because he wanted the peanut butter to be crunchy, and I refused on principle."

Vince gasps in mock disgust. "You like *smooth* peanut butter?"

"You like *crunchy* peanut butter?" I balk. "I think we've made a grave mistake here."

"I'll turn around right now," he teasingly threatens but makes no move to do so.

I reach across the center console to slip my hand in his. "What time does the movie start?"

"Well, we have a few options, but I was wondering if we could stop by a party at Bill's before we go?" He squeezes my palm, likely predicting my discomfort. "I tried to get out of it, but Bill gave me this whole lecture about team bonding and how, since I'm the captain, I need to be there."

"Oh," I breathe.

It's not exactly what I envisioned for our first grand evening together.

"Is that okay?"

"Sure," I say nonchalantly, trying to mask my disappointment. "We'll be quick, though, right?"

"Definitely," Vince confirms. "I want you all to myself."

"What about all the other people in the theater?" I ask innocently.

"I *guess* they're invited. But we're not sharing our popcorn with them."

"Fair enough." I reach into my bag, pulling out the gigantic bag of M&M's I picked up from the gas station earlier. "At least I have contraband."

He laughs. "I like the way you think."

When we arrive to the house, I'm relieved the scene is

much more lowkey than the party Andy dragged me to after Homecoming, but unfortunately, there seems to be much more testosterone, chugging, and chanting.

I haven't exactly *been* to a soccer party so much as I've heard about them and eavesdropped on them from my bedroom.

As we cross into the living room, Vince is pulled into the crowd of his teammates, and he offers me an apologetic look as our grip falters.

I stand awkwardly without purpose or a person to talk to, but I see the other girls in attendance—only three others—huddled on the couch.

I join them, glad that they're steering clear of the boys' antics, but they don't make an effort to include me in their conversation. And having never spoken to any of them before, I feel like the odd woman out.

"How's it going?" I ask the girl beside me.

She either doesn't hear me or pretends I haven't opened my mouth.

Judging by the way the others pointedly avoid the eye contact I'm trying to make, they seem to want nothing to do with me.

I try my hardest not to consider why, and so I keep my attention on Vince, just like I've done so many other times since school started.

He denies every drink that's handed to him, blocking out invitations and encouragements with the crossing of his arms on his chest.

Time drags on as I check my phone again and again, watching an entire hour pass by rather slowly.

Just for something to do, I stand up, smoothing down

the front of my dress to go seek out the bathroom, but I'm pulled into the huddle of guys by Bill.

"Maren Montgomery," he slurs, pushing me deeper into their circle. "So honored you chose to grace us with your presence."

I've never spoken to him until this evening, but I know his face from photographing the team. He's the one who originally explained to Vince who I am—or rather, who I'm related to.

I try to break out of his grasp as I look for Vince, but his meaty fingers grip my wrist.

With this impressive hand strength, he should definitely be a goalkeeper.

Bill smiles at me widely with unfocused eyes. "Soccer royalty has arrived, boys," he says sarcastically. "Cheers!"

They all raise their cups.

It might be a nice gesture if it were genuine, but nearly all the echoes are mocking, and at least half of Bill's beer spills down the front of my dress.

I jump back and grimace as he chugs the liquid down, completely unaware he's given me a beer shower.

When I vowed to open myself up, I knew I'd feel a range of emotions from fury to heartache, but I never thought I would experience this level of embarrassment.

It's not necessarily from the big show that was just put on in my "honor" or even the fact that the fabric of my dress is rapidly soaking up sticky beer; it's how excited I let myself get for my night with Vince.

I guess one positive is the bar for any dates moving forward has been set exceptionally low, given my experience with guys is nonexistent.

Andy and I were each other's first kiss—something we're both equally appalled and entertained by—and the only boyfriend I've ever had was in middle school, with our only interaction being slow dancing a foot apart at the monthly dances in the gym.

Really, it's my own fault for having grand ideas about how magical tonight would be.

I force my way through the rowdy group and catch the smirking eyes of the girls on the couch as I grab my coat and dash through the front door.

Vince finally catches up with me on the sidewalk as my shaky fingers slide across my phone screen.

"I'm so sorry," he says, taking in my ruined dress and angry expression.

I ignore his apology and pull up Andy's number.

"Maren, I'm sorry," he repeats and steps around to my line of sight, trying to console me. "I didn't mean for this to happen. Obviously. It's just—"

"Do you know why I'm angry?" I cut in, not interested in hearing him grovel. "Really angry?"

Vince steps away from me, giving me room to breathe and let my frustration out.

"Because my brother did every single thing his team-mates ever wanted," I bite out, letting my emotions run free. "And look where it got him."

I seethe, uncaring that some parents lead their kids across the street to ignore my wrath.

"He didn't even want to go to that stupid party," I rant. "He called me on the way, saying he'd wanted to get an early start on driving to come home and attend one of my indoor games, but he couldn't bear to let the team down."

I tug at the ends of my hair, watching Vince's face fall.

"You know how it goes," I continue. "They want you to show up. They want you to drink. They want you to take turns running and jumping in the freezing cold lake because it's *team bonding*, but then..." My voice breaks. "Then you never resurface."

Vince reaches out, and I let him bring me into his arms.

He tugs me flush against his chest, holding me while rubbing my back, and I note how the front of his clothes are getting soaked with our proximity.

After what feels like an eternity, I calm down and pull back.

"I really am sorry, Maren," Vince says quietly. "I would have never brought you here if I knew they were going to treat you like that. Honestly."

From everything I know about him, I know that to be true—or at least, I know he wants it to be.

But it doesn't mean that tonight wasn't a massive letdown.

I sigh. "I believe you."

"Maren," he says slowly, renewing his grip on my arms. "I'm glad you opened up and told me, but I wish it was under different circumstances. I wish this whole night was different."

"Me too."

"We can still make the next showing. I think I have a change of clothes in my car, if you don't mind a clean kit?"

I smile sadly. "I think I'll pass."

He nods and looks a little devastated. "I'll just take you home."

I shake my head, and I see a glimmer of hope in his eyes.

"Can you drop me at Andy's, please?" I clarify.

His expression falters. "Sure," he says after a pause.

More than anything at the moment, even more than a shower and a set of clean clothes, I need my best friend.

NINETEEN

Andy, unlike Vince, has absolutely no tolerance for my beer-scented self.

When I arrive, he gives me a once-over and shoves me toward his bathroom, depositing a towel and a clean pair of sweats on the counter before shutting me in.

"I ordered pizza," he says when I join him on the couch after I've cleaned off and pulled my hair up in a messy bun.

I nod. "Did you—"

"Get green peppers and pineapple on it?" he interrupts with an eyeroll. "Yes. Even though they're both disgusting, you seem to really need it."

"Thank you," I say. "You must really love me if you're willing to endure that to make me feel better."

Andy sinks lower into the couch and props his feet up on the coffee table. "Obviously. Now, spill why you're here with me instead of having some fabulous night with Vince Novak?"

I spend the better part of an hour sharing every detail.

He listens at attention and only interrupts to answer the door for the delivery guy and clarify something for whatever mental picture of my failed date he is building in his mind.

"In conclusion," Andy says, picking a green pepper off his pizza slice with a look of disgust. "I'm going to have to dump all the itching powder in the world into the boys' soccer uniforms before their next game as payback."

I giggle. "Not necessary, but I'll enjoy the thought of that every time I see Bill at practice."

"And you didn't recognize the girls on the couch? Because I'm sure I'd know *something* about at least one of them I could put to use—"

"Andy, I'm not out for blood," I tell him. "I'm just disappointed."

"Right," he says, brushing crust crumbs back into the box. "If anything, I should be putting my energy toward verbally slapping Vince across the face."

"As much as I would like to see you take my side regarding Vince for once, you probably shouldn't."

Andy quirks an eyebrow. "What do you mean *for once?*"

"Oh, come on, you've been rooting for him this whole time. Winking at him across the cafeteria, dropping sly little hints to me about him, and you even gave him my phone number."

"I didn't do it for *Vince*," he scoffs. "I think he's one of the good ones, and he genuinely likes you, Maren. And, since you've been spending more time with him, you seem..."

"Better?" I prompt.

"No." Andy shakes his head. "That implies you weren't

good before. You've always been good, Maren, great, the best, even. You've just been dealing with your demons in your own way. But as your best friend, I've taken a vow—"

I laugh. "A whole vow?"

"Don't interrupt me. I'm monologuing." But even he can't hide his smile. "It's my duty to do things in your best interest, like encourage you to open up to some handsome soccer player who looks at you like you're a trophy or a gold medal or a World Cup, or whatever it is people like him put on a pedestal."

"Well, technically, it's not a cup that's given out to the winners, it's the name of the tourn—"

When he levels his stare on me, I stop.

"I get what you're saying," I relent.

"So, as a final note on this topic before we switch to gossiping while watching trashy reality TV, I say you should just enjoy the inevitable groveling that he's going to do to apologize and move on."

I nod. "I think I can do that."

After following Andy's exact plan for our evening, we fall asleep on the sofa, kicking each other and fighting over the blanket throughout the night.

When my alarm goes off early the next morning, I take the advice Vince once gave me—sneak in before my parents wake up in the morning, not wait until the dead of night to accidentally scare a family member.

Andy drops me back at home without consequence, then I crawl into my own bed. At a more reasonable hour, I toss my beer-stained dress in the laundry before digging through the freezer for something edible.

The doorbell rings as I'm tossing the stick from my

cherry popsicle into the garbage, and I peek out the window to see Vince standing on the doorstep with a sizable bouquet in his hands.

I guess this is what Andy meant by "inevitable groveling," but I really wish it was happening on school grounds instead of my front porch.

My parents have been locked in my dad's office all morning, so my only hope is to get rid of Vince as quickly as I can.

Before I open the door, I catch sight of my stained mouth in the mirror, then try—and fail—to wipe it clean with the back of my hand.

"Hey," I say quickly.

"Hey," he returns. "These are for you."

The bouquet is a beautiful mix of purples, oranges, and yellows.

I wonder how long I can keep them in my room until my parents notice.

He offers a sheepish smile. "I figured I should come by with a formal apology, but I know it's a little cheesy."

"I like cheesy," I admit, bringing the flowers up to my nose.

Although I'm partial to Vince's citrus scent, these smell divine.

His gaze drops to my feet.

And it's then I notice I'm still wearing Andy's borrowed clothes, consisting of tight sweatpants tucked into high socks, a cropped shirt, and an oversized zip-up sweatshirt.

I blush at his amusement. "If you wait out here for just a second, I'll—"

"Maren?"

I flinch at the sound of my mother's voice, and Vince doesn't miss it.

"Why don't you head home, and I'll call you in a bit," I suggest lightly, moving to close the door on him.

"You don't want me to meet your parents?" he asks, hurt palpable in his voice.

I grimace. "Sorry, it's not you. I'll explain later."

Just as I'm about to close the door, my mother steps into the entryway.

"Maren, who is it?"

Vince tears his eyes away from her and glances at me, seeking permission to introduce himself.

I shrug as I grip the vase with my fingertips and wish I had a better shield.

"Hello, Mrs. Montgomery, I'm Vince Novak." He puts on his most charming grin. "It's so wonderful to finally meet you."

She blinks and accepts his outstretched hand while I watch the emotion roll over her.

First, there's disbelief.

Then, curiosity at the bouquet in my hands.

And, finally, I see the recognition of an opportunity to dive right back into the past.

"Come in, won't you?" she says to him sweetly.

"Oh, no," I protest. "Vince actually has to get going now."

"Nonsense," she insists, waving him inside.

I'm speechless at her pleasant attitude, given how often she and my father spoke of Vince in stressed, hushed tones.

It seems that has been momentarily forgotten or maybe

I've completely misunderstood everything about my parents—but I know the latter is certainly not true.

Still, it's strange, though, that all it takes is one introduction for my mother to transform into a person I haven't seen in years.

She's the eager hostess, chatting up Vince on his recent games, asking about any injuries or hardships he's been working through, and pressing him for details on his future.

And then it hits me.

This whole thing is a sad attempt to replicate the Jake-sized void in her life.

I don't know whether to cry or scream, so I merely sit silently across from him at the kitchen table, keeping my eyes on the flowers my mother insisted I put at the center, and they go back and forth in complete conversational ease until my father arrives.

"Who's this?"

Vince balks at the gruff voice, likely taken aback by the similarities between my father and Uncle Eric, but he quickly recovers and stands up to greet him.

"Vince brought Maren flowers this morning," my mother explains, beaming. "Thoughtfully already placed in a vase. No pesky stem trimming required!"

My father hums. "Well, that certainly explains her recent photography projects," he says.

I grind my teeth.

"Oh?" Vince asks, glancing at me in confusion. "What has she shown you?"

"A very...interesting calendar," my mother supplies.

"I'm really excited for it to come out," Vince tells her. "I think it's going to raise a lot of money."

My mother's brows pull together. "For what?"

After another glance at me, Vince explains, "Maren and I teamed up to raise money for the art program. Some of the funding got cut to help pay for a new ticket booth, among other things."

"A new ticket booth? Didn't they just replace it when Jake..." My father stops himself and clears his throat. "A few years ago?"

Vince shrugs. "I'm not sure, exactly—"

"Oh, you know what, I have a hilarious picture of Maren in front of that very same booth," my mother boasts.

Our collective gaze follows her as she rushes into the living room to grab a photo album that hasn't seen the light of day since before Jake died.

"Here it is," she says proudly, pressing it down in front of Vince. "She was such a little ball hog when she played, but she was good. I mean *really* good. If only she'd stuck with it instead of spending all her time on this hobby, she could have made something of herself."

"But her photography is incredible," Vince argues.

My mother waves a dismissive hand. "We're a soccer family, through and through. Vince, tell me more about your style of play. Of course, we've all read the papers, but I'm curious how you've liked being coached by my brother-in-law?"

Fed up with her crap, I finally look at Vince and tilt my head toward the door, trying to signal it's time to get the hell out of here.

Thankfully, he picks up on my silent plea.

"Actually, I'm so sorry, but Maren and I have plans," he says with a false frown. "In fact, we'd better get going."

My mother takes in my very shabby appearance. "Right now?"

"Uh huh," I answer as I step into a pair of slides. "I'll be back later."

Before they can argue or do something even more embarrassing, I push Vince toward the front door, not breathing until I'm buckled in his front seat.

To his credit, Vince doesn't say a word as he drives over to North Park.

But I see him piecing together every single thing I haven't told him, and I'm content to let him process in silence.

Once he parks the car, I jump out, and we walk wordlessly but hand in hand to the same little area of trees we visited before my film camera broke.

"So, everything is starting to make more sense," he finally says.

I nod, smiling tightly. "All my secrets are out now."

"Oh, I think you're more complex than that," Vince says.

"Maybe I'm not," I mumble.

He pulls me into him, rubbing my back to warm me up.

I exhale and relax into him, memorizing the feel of his hands on my body.

"If it'll make you feel better, I have another secret I'm willing to share," he murmurs in my ear.

"What is it?" I ask nervously.

"I really, really, really want to kiss you."

I swallow, and I'm sure he can hear it, given his proximity to my neck.

My heart pounds as he pulls back to look me in the eyes, questioning if he has permission, and at my slight nod, his lips meet mine.

I gasp at the way his soft lips make my entire body tingle.

Vince pulls back and smiles before he moves again, touching the exposed skin of my waist.

Despite the warmth of his touch, I shiver, completely overwhelmed by him.

He's gentle, moving slowly to give my body time to calibrate to all these new feelings.

The rhythm between us is intoxicating, far more effective than the beer I tried, and I slide my hands up his muscular arms, then grip his shoulders for leverage until I'm on my toes, pressing up against him, reaching for more.

How have I made it almost eighteen years of my life without feeling like this?

I don't realize how breathless I am until he pulls away, dropping his forehead to mine as we greedily inhale oxygen.

"Maren?" Vince whispers.

"Yeah," I return, slightly delirious.

"You taste like cherry."

I grin.

Andy was right—cherry is the flavor of happy, after all.

TWENTY

The calendars *finally* arrive the following week, and they're a massive success.

I'm a little ashamed I'm not even that excited.

Things are still a little awkward with Mr. Wilde, and while his existence doesn't solely tether my loyalty to the arts program, my focus elsewhere has made me realize it's not everything in the world to me anymore.

An announcement at school names Vince and me as the brains behind the collaborative operation, which is a little embarrassing, but luckily, it happens during the final period of the day, so I can lock myself in the darkroom after to distract myself from all the attention.

Once there, I have just enough time to wrench apart my broken camera and try to salvage the film inside before I have to head over to Vince's game and photograph it, so I get lost in the chemical process of bringing my photos to life.

I didn't get to use the entire roll before the camera

broke, but under the red light, I can tell the used film appears to be undamaged.

As I process each negative, I'm reminded that Vince is the perfect subject, looking somehow at ease even though he's posing.

That is, until I get him to smile with a few close-up shots.

The progression of his grin is revealed as I hang up the end results side by side to dry.

My heart flutters at how he's depicted in that final moment, but my good mood falters when I start developing the picture he took of me and recall the memory.

He stands, blocking out the sun in the sky, and I meet his gaze, challenging him to pick out the perfect shot based on my own logic.

The sound of the shutter releasing from this side of the camera makes me gasp slightly.

And then this moment between us is officially solidified into permanence.

"What is my little flaw?" I ask lightly as he reaches out to help me up.

When our skin touches, I swear it's electric and magical and so many things all at once.

Vince returns my camera once I've brushed myself off. "You'll see when you develop the film."

My face in the photo, by an objective standard, is perfect.

It was a good skin day for me—not one single pimple made an appearance—and I look natural in the setting, sprawled out among the fall foliage.

But I see what he wanted me to see.

My eyes.

They're the perfect amount of open—my lids aren't blown too wide, despite the gasp I gave before he clicked the button—but there's a sadness in their dark depths that's so visceral it overtakes everything else.

All the times I've looked at my own reflection, I've never caught this detail before, but it's right before my very eyes.

What's especially baffling to me is that, in the past few weeks, Vince has made me happier than anyone else, and yet, even in his presence, I'm somehow suffocating myself.

I sigh and check the time, knowing I'm cutting it close to the game, but instead of rushing off to the stadium, I dash to the bathroom.

I stand in front of the mirror, tilting my chin at different angles until I stare at myself head-on.

What Vince captured is still there, but I'm relieved to see it's lessened dramatically—a testament to the promise I made to try and offload my inner burdens.

I trace the lines of my cheekbones before rubbing my temples, wishing the physical relief of tension worked on my mental state, too.

I fluff my hair out of a vain habit, then set off toward the game, which has just kicked off.

From the few minutes of play I witness as I approach, I can see this is going to be one of those intense back and forth games.

If I were watching as a fan, I'd certainly be chewing my nails down to nothing. Through the lens of my camera, though, I'm able to simultaneously pull away from the suspense and laser-focus on the details.

My favorite snap of the first half is when the other

team's defender misses a slide tackle, and Vince chips the ball over him and presses forward before passing the ball easily to Bill, who scores.

The game is combative, with rampant insults and yellow cards flashing every few minutes. When there are five minutes left on the clock, the score is tied.

Then Vince is fouled just outside the box.

Chaos erupts, with both sides screaming at the referee, who waves everyone off and signals for Vince to take a free kick. The other team creates a wall of defense, and Vince lines up.

After a breath, he gingerly steps forward and takes his shot.

The ball soars through the air and curves, missing the goalkeeper's hand by mere inches before it hits the back of the net, near the upper corner.

Vince's teammates lose it, going absolutely wild, and so do the assistant coaches and the crowd.

The only two people who don't have a reaction are Uncle Eric and me. I'm distracted by my camera, and my uncle is likely considering what criticism to offer Vince post-game.

But we officially get the win, meaning Greene's undefeated season is still alive.

I wait for Vince in the parking lot, leaning against my car as he completes his post-game interview and showers off.

"Hey," he says upon his arrival, shuffling his bag on his shoulder so he can bring me into his arms.

"Good game," I tell him after he releases me. "It was a close one, though."

"Well, I actually have a theory on that."

"Oh?" I breathe as he unzips his bag.

"I know you don't have much patience for this type of stuff, but I do hear it's good luck for a player's girlfriend to wear his jersey on game day," Vince says casually, pulling out a freshly laundered one and handing it over.

The material floats between us, waiting for me to accept the gesture and the title.

He quirks his brow as if challenging me to object.

I wonder what he sees in my eyes in that moment—the terrified, somewhat glassy expression he documented with my own lens or the exhilaration I feel about the future I'm starting to build toward?

It doesn't matter, though, because when I grip the jersey in my palm, I lean up to kiss him with my eyes closed and my heart open.

TWENTY-ONE

I get to wear Vince's jersey for the first time the following Thursday.

The stares as I enter each class catch me off guard, and it makes me want to peel the jersey off my back. But seeing me in it makes Vince grin the entire lunch period, so I don't back out on my agreement to wear it.

Mr. Wilde eyes the name on my back warily as he sits down beside me.

I glance up at him from my computer, where I've been studying my shots from last weekend to see if any are portfolio-worthy, and offer him a tight smile. "Mr. Wilde."

He inches closer. "You know it's 'Owen' when we're alone," he reminds me in a low voice.

I turn, noting how all the other students are out of earshot and engrossed in their projects.

The privilege of calling him by his first name used to make me feel so mature and chic, like he was more of a friend than anything else. But something broke when he made comments about Vince and me, and I haven't made an effort to repair it.

I wonder if this is his attempt to smooth things over. After all, it was Vince and I who saved his job for another semester.

"Abigail called me about tonight's gallery show," Mr. Wilde says. "You're going, right?"

"Yes, of course," I tell him.

I don't add that I've had this date in the back of my mind ever since she emailed me about it.

"And you're going alone?" he presses, eyeing my clothing once again.

"Yes," I admit.

Even if Vince didn't have an away game tonight, I'm not sure I'm allowed to bring a plus one—and I don't want to come off as rude or entitled by asking to bring my boyfriend.

"Good," he breathes. "Because a few of us are going out to dinner after the event, and you'll want to meet these people. Editors of design magazines, other artists, and even a private collector. It would be really good for you, and for your career, if you got to know them."

He's dangling this opportunity that sounds too good to be true, and I hate myself for being unable to turn it down.

I chew on my bottom lip. "Okay."

"I'll pick you up at seven," he says as the bell rings, then turns to address the rest of the class. "I'll want each of you to give me a rundown tomorrow of where you're at in your projects."

As I stare at the back of Vince's head in history class next period, I feel oddly guilty at the agreement I made with Mr. Wilde. Like I'm somehow compromising my morals for the opportunity to network with people whose names I don't even know.

I reluctantly shrug off his jersey when I get home, annoyed it smells more like my lavender body wash than his citrus scent, and stare at my closet.

I should call Andy in for assistance, but I'm already feeling put off enough about the entire situation that I don't want to subject myself to his teasing.

Eventually, I settle on the same black dress I wore to the art fundraiser and try to dress it up as much as I can with my sole pair of high heels and the statement earrings Andy got me for Christmas last year.

My parents still aren't home when Mr. Wilde pulls up in his vintage convertible—it seems like a very *him* car but also impractical for the upcoming winter weather.

At least the top is up tonight.

We have mostly one-sided chitchat on the way to the gallery.

He fills me in on some of the major players who are expected to attend, as well as some background on Abigail Archer.

They met in Paris when she was on vacation a few years ago, and she allegedly liked his work enough to ask him to be part of one of her upcoming collections.

Not only is she a collector and curator but she's also very big into philanthropy, working with several charities around the city to keep art alive and flourishing in schools.

I'm dying to ask why he didn't go to her for help instead of putting the financial burden of the Greene arts program on the students, but I'm actively trying to not be combative or anything other than a student companion.

Because in addition to slight nerves over meeting so many people in this circle, I'm also overthinking every thought I've ever had about Mr. Wilde.

I was so blindly infatuated by his presence and his opinion of my work that my perception of him was skewed.

I once thought his laid-back nature was appealing, like he was on another level of cool that I couldn't even begin to comprehend, but as he leads me inside the beautiful gallery, I compare him to his peers, and my expectation of him is dramatically lowered.

With a glass of champagne in his hand, he regales the other attendees with the same stories I've heard for years. Only, for this new, captive audience, he exaggerates the details, lapping up how they laugh.

I drift away while he's distracted, content to take in each piece on display at my own pace.

At first, I don't see the central theme, but after a few steps, I catch the common thread and smile to myself.

There are a variety of pieces and forms, some ceramics, some metal artwork that winds up the walls, but in the middle of the gallery, lit up on display, is a gigantic painting of a beautiful girl.

"What do you think it means?" a woman standing beside me asks, her eyes on the piece.

She's dressed pristinely, and the light reflects off her sheet of golden blonde hair, making her look like some sort of angel.

I wish it were socially appropriate for me to take out my

camera and snap a photo of her, but I simply tear my eyes away and focus on the canvas.

The subject of the painting looks about my age, crafted beautifully in long slashes of black and white. Toward the bottom of the piece, I see her hands clutching a beautiful depiction of a heart that's vibrant in all shades of red.

At first glance, it looks like she's cupping the heart so forcefully that the life is being squeezed out of it. But as I blink, I notice it's the opposite—the heart is so full, it's almost escaping the cavern it's contained in, and this girl is the keeper of it.

I scan the room, and I think I see why Abigail Archer might be interested in my photography.

"I think all these pieces aren't what they appear on the surface," I tell the woman.

She nods, revealing nothing else. "How so?"

"Well, originally when I looked at this painting, I thought the artist was trying to show how someone else has a hold on their heart, literally and figuratively, but the more I take in the details, the more clearly I see the gentleness of the subject's hands, how eager and kind her eyes are. I don't think she's meant to be the one stifling anyone...I think she's doing the saving."

"I see it that way, too," she agrees slowly before turning to face me.

"Cool." I nod because I don't know what else to say.

But I internally cringe at how juvenile I sound.

"I didn't catch your name."

"Oh, I'm Maren," I tell her, holding out a hand.

"Montgomery, I assume?" she asks, accepting the gesture.

My brows pull together.

"I'm Abigail Archer, and it's so wonderful to finally meet you."

I feel my eyes widen in surprise. "Oh, yes, I've been—"

"There you are," Mr. Wilde says, approaching us. "Abigail, you're a dream as always."

"Thank you, Owen," she returns. "Your brilliant student and I were just looking over one of my son's pieces."

My jaw drops open. "Your son painted this?"

She nods. "It was his way of telling his now-fiancée that he loved her. Although it means a lot to both of them, they don't have any room for it in their tiny Brooklyn apartment, so I get to be the keeper of it for now."

"Abigail has a habit of collecting things no one else wants," Owen teases. "Like me, for instance."

She smiles at him but doesn't fall for his attempt at charm. "Oh, I think you do just fine for yourself."

If I didn't like this woman so much already, her response would have done me in completely.

"Maren, I would still really like to review your portfolio," she tells me. "Since I'm officially back in town, let's coordinate a date to do so. Just message me at the address you have, and we'll put something on the calendar."

"Yes, yes," I say eagerly. "Thank you so much."

She winks at me. "Well, I should do some rounds. Enjoy the evening."

"Bye, Abigail," Owen says to her as she leaves, then grins. "You can thank me when you're a big, famous photographer."

The exhilaration I felt in speaking to her falls flat at his implication that I owe him something when all he did was brag to her about my work—likely crediting himself in some way while doing so—and hand me a business card.

"I will forever be grateful for the introduction to her and for the help you've given me with my photography," I say to him with forced politeness.

Even though, aside from working to create the dark-room and planting the seed about my talent, he really hasn't done much to improve my actual skill.

"Well, sure, your photos are good, but it's not just that, Maren. You're the complete package."

"What do you mean?" I ask tentatively.

He takes another sip of champagne and puts his hand on my back, steering me around the gallery.

"It means that all these pieces are good, but the artist has something else to offer," he says. "People don't buy my paintings because they like the way I smear paint on the canvas. They buy into the Owen Wilde experience."

I blink. "I'm not sure that's true."

He laughs at my apparent ignorance.

"What about people who buy from a gallery without ever meeting you?" I argue.

"They are going off the recommendation of someone I've met previously or trusting the instincts of whoever is spreading the word about me," he answers easily. "They're buying into the idea of me because someone else told them I was worth a damn."

"So you think because you've vouched for me with Abigail, I have an in on making a career for myself?" I ask him plainly.

He nods. "And so it begins."

I let out a breath and demand, "Why?"

"Why what?" Mr. Wilde balks.

"Why did you take an interest in me?" I press. "Out of every student who came through your classes, why me?"

He chuckles and waves for a server to trade his empty champagne flute for a full one. "Look at yourself in a mirror, Maren. You know you're gorgeous, but you're also so broken. The package together...how you're tied up in a bow while the box itself is cracked...is art."

It's the strangest compliment I've ever received.

And I'm deeply offended by it.

"You think I'm *pretty*, so you decided to help me?"

"We both know it's more than that," he murmurs, running a finger down my bare arm.

I shiver.

And it's not in the good, thrilling way Vince causes me to do so.

"Well, if that's the case," I rasp, "I think I'll pass."

He blinks. "What are you talking about?"

"I don't need you to vouch for me or take me to dinners or introduce me to anyone," I hiss. "I'll figure it out on my own."

"Maren," he calls, but I'm already on my way out.

I grab my coat from the rack and storm outside, brushing past a startled Abigail.

I run as fast as I can in my heels until I'm certain Mr. Wilde isn't following me, and then I let my rage turn into tears as I call Andy and beg him to come pick me up.

TWENTY-TWO

"So, you're really not going to tell Vince?" Andy asks me for what seems like the fifteenth time on our way to the guidance counselor's office.

I thought my best friend would be good moral support, but it appears I was wrong.

All he seems to want to do is pester me about my boyfriend—the same one who, just a few weeks ago, he was very angry with.

Time heals all wounds, I guess.

For people who aren't me, at least.

"No," I tell him with a hint of exasperation. "He's got a lot on his mind with the postseason approaching, I don't want to burden him."

Andy scowls. "I don't think that's a good idea."

"I've got it," I tell him, feigning confidence I wish I felt.

The truth is that after everything Vince went through with his sister, he doesn't need to deal with this. I'm protecting him from reliving a nightmare scenario, but obviously, Andy doesn't know the details. It's not my story to tell.

And, honestly, my interaction with Mr. Wilde is so embarrassingly tame compared to Vince's sister's situation that I don't want to get into all of it with him. It's not worth the burden.

Really, I should have just put my foot down and driven *myself* to the gallery, which would have likely changed the course of the entire night's events. More importantly, Andy would have no idea, and I wouldn't be taking a guilt trip right now for handling it on my own.

"I'll meet you in the cafeteria when I'm done," I tell him, waving him off.

"And when Vince wonders where his girlfriend is?" Andy asks. "Why she's not in the cafeteria, ready to rehash last night's game?"

"You can tell him where I am but not the details of why," I relent.

"I don't like this, Maren."

I huff. "Best friend code of secrecy, please?"

Andy rolls his eyes. "You made that up just now."

"But it's working, right?" I ask him with a sardonic smile.

He sighs, then pulls me in for a brief hug.

"I hope you know what you're doing," he says in my ear. "And if you don't, that's okay. I'm here for you. Just don't hold it all in, okay?"

"Thanks," I say, shrugging him off.

He doesn't get it.

This situation isn't even all that draining.

It's mostly just mortifying.

I'm ready for it to be over, and I don't want to deal with more of Andy's reassurance, Vince's worry, or Mr. Wilde's lechery. I just need to continue down the path I'm on, pressing ahead with my camera in hand.

But first, I need to drop out of my art class.

It'll be easy enough—a paper signature and a few clicks of a button on a screen and my schedule change will be complete.

But of course, like all things in my life, it is *not*, in fact, easy.

I spend twenty minutes pleading my case to the guidance counselor, who won't budge without explanation. The notoriety I gained getting my photos published in *The Review*, along with my work in fundraising with the calendars, hasn't gone unnoticed by the department.

And it's why Mr. Harvey doesn't understand why such a "promising young student" would be so eager to drop out of the class that is fostering their growth.

I tiptoe around the issue, saying I would be more productive in study hall.

He definitely doesn't buy it, but he does slide a permission form into my hands.

"You need a parent or guardian to sign this," he says.

"But—"

He narrows his eyes at me. "Non-negotiable."

I frown and clutch it between my fingers.

"Thank you," I say coolly.

As I leave his office, I try to figure out how to spin this to my parents.

No matter how I start a conversation with them, it ends poorly, regardless of the topic.

But I can't even imagine how they'll react to the news of me dropping a class, even if it's one they weren't thrilled with me taking in the first place.

I know one angle I could take, but giving them hope that I'm giving up photography might be as bad as secretly continuing on with it, and I'm just not in the headspace to deal with all that at the moment.

As I'm walking, taking the long way back to the cafeteria to avoid Jake's photo, inspiration strikes. Mr. Harvey said parent *or guardian,* and it just so happens I have a blood relation in the building.

My pace quickens as I turn and cut directly through to the athletic office, ignoring my brother's eyes as I enter.

"Maren," Uncle Eric says, glancing up from his computer in surprise. "Is everything okay?"

I nod and take a seat in front of his desk. "I was wondering if I could ask a favor."

"Of course. What can I do?"

I hand over the piece of paper, realizing I need to figure out what lie to spin.

He reads it quickly, too fast for me to scramble a story together, then meets my eyes with a curious expression. "You want to drop out of art class? Why?"

The flimsy excuse I gave Mr. Harvey is definitely not going to work with my uncle, and I didn't think to prepare a different one in the time it took me to arrive here.

"I, uh…"

Uncle Eric sighs as he sits back, pinching the bridge of his nose between his thumb and pointer finger.

His reaction startles me, like I'm dropping some huge,

heavy burden in his lap instead of a piece of paper that will take him about two seconds to sign.

"I saw you the other week," he says evenly. "With Vince, on the field."

I swallow and nod, even though this isn't news, because I thought he'd be pleased rather than pained watching that event unfold.

"Seeing you in the stadium with a camera in your hand has been fun for me, but watching you sprint downfield...it was something I never thought I'd witness again."

He sits up and places his elbows on the desk, leaning toward me.

"If things were different, if Jake were still alive, I can't help but think you would have grown to totally outshine him."

The thickness in my throat startles me, as do the hot tears that trickle down my face.

I came here on my high horse, in complete control of my life and emotions, and the last thing I expected was to be tossed into whatever this is.

"I thought maybe being close to the sport again would help bridge the gap and that you'd come back to play," he admits. "But I've made peace with how wrong I was. Frankly, I was just happy to see you again. I can tell how passionate you are about your photography. It's as natural as you look on the field, so it's odd to see you even for a second without a camera in your hand."

He stops and forces my gaze.

"So I'm just confused why you're suddenly eager to give it all up," he says seriously. "Help me understand, Maren."

"I'm not giving it up," I promise, my voice shaking.

He slides the paper back across the table. "Looks to me like you are."

I open and close my mouth, wondering how to salvage this conversation.

As I think, Uncle Eric takes a deep breath.

"I'm ashamed at how long it has taken me to cope with losing Jake," he says distantly. "And that it took me even longer to realize I've lost you in the process. I can't do that anymore, Maren. You're my niece, and I love you. I want to see you succeed, so I can't enable you to sabotage yourself with this. It's selfish, I know, but it hurts too much to watch you do this to yourself."

My chest constricts so tightly that each breath hurts, and my brain is in such a loop that I can't come up with one single word in defense of myself.

Instead, I stand on weakened knees, clutching the form, and leave.

Like a coward.

And not at all who I'm trying to be.

I barely make it into the hallway before I sink down to the floor.

I'm still within eyeshot of Jake's picture, which makes me feel one thousand times worse. It's a reminder that his life and death have had—and still have—such a hold on me. I can't even escape my predatory art teacher without having a conversation about my dead brother.

I wonder if it's going to take me completely escaping this town and hiding my identity to finally be free.

"What's wrong?"

Of course.

Just what I need right now is for Vince to jog down the

hallway and catch me in this awful state of snot and emotion.

"Nothing," I say quickly, sitting up and wiping my face.

He kneels down beside me, cupping the side of my face as he gently tilts my chin and takes me in.

I shrug his hands off.

Even though he means well, the gesture of him controlling where my eyes land makes me want to run like hell.

"This doesn't seem like nothing," he says lightly.

I wrap my arms around my knees, trying to hold it together. "I really don't want to talk about it."

Vince watches me curl into myself, then sighs. "You're clearly not okay, and I want to help—"

"I don't need your help, Vince," I say gently.

He frowns. "I thought we were past all the secrets, Maren."

"This isn't a secret," I protest, seeing the line of his jaw harden in disappointment.

"Then tell me."

I shake my head and press my lips firmly together, holding onto my resolve as my irritation grows.

Why can't he just drop this?

"It's just something I don't want to talk about," I tell him.

"But that's what I'm here for, Maren, to listen and support you and—"

"I know, Vince," I snap. "I get it. You're you, all perfect, and I'm me, so damn broken that I'm shattered, and you just want to fix it."

"I don't think you need fixing, Maren," Vince says quietly.

I huff. "Well, I just don't want to talk about it, Vince. Just leave it alone."

He stands up and backs away, nodding. "Well, I guess, just let me know when you do."

I force my gaze back to the ground, not watching him retreat, and let out a low string of curse words.

I stay in this exact position through art class, purposely ditching, and try to pull myself together enough that I can sit in the back of the history classroom.

For once, I'm almost grateful to go right home after the last bell rings. I feel so drained that, when I arrive, it doesn't even hurt—physically or emotionally—to show my parents the form and simply ask if they can sign it.

Like Uncle Eric, they surprise me with their reactions.

"That's great," my mother says with a grin. "Finally giving it up to focus on more important things."

My father nods in approval and agreement. "Is there another elective you can take instead?"

"Oh, I wonder if Mrs. Spine is still teaching the senior-level business course?"

I indulge their behavior and half-listen to their speculation on other possible career routes for me.

I don't say a word, simply taking in how happy they are that I'm giving up something I love so dearly.

When I deflate completely and can't listen for another minute, I go up to my room and curl up on my bed with Vince's jersey and my shame.

TWENTY-THREE

Normally, if I want to avoid the world, I'd have the safety of my darkroom to hide in. But the day after I drop out of art class and club, I see the janitor tearing down the black cloth and removing the setup from the converted closet.

I'm just glad I didn't leave anything behind because surely my work would end up in the trash.

But maybe that's where it belongs at this point.

My emotional turmoil has robbed me of all my creativity, but I'm still obligated to keep up my end of the bargain with *The Review*, photographing Vince, which is pure torture.

He continues to sit at our lunch table, chatting up Andy and Michael, and sends me exasperated looks, waiting for me to break the barrier between us.

But I'm not letting anyone in at the moment—not even Andy, who I swear texts me every hour.

I'm not boxing everyone out simply for the sake of doing so.

If I've learned anything about myself these past few months, it's that I can figure it all out on my own.

I can work through my disappointment with how things turned out with Owen, stand on my own two feet to revive my passion for photography without Vince as a muse, and even navigate the complex relationship I have with my parents, which is suddenly flourishing.

As a bonus, I've become an exceptionally productive student.

I've traded my camera for homework, and that's usually what I focus on during lunch now, solving problems and doing worksheets while Andy, Michael, and Vince carry on a conversation easily enough without me.

As I start on my rough draft for an English paper, I jot down the date and gasp, noting it's first postseason game for Vince and the rest of his team.

I swallow before I lift my gaze and scan the cafeteria. The girls from Bill's awful party are all wearing their boyfriends' jerseys.

I still sleep with Vince's every single night—which is pathetic on so many levels—but I'm definitely not wearing it right now.

When I bring my attention back to the table, I lock eyes with Vince and immediately see his sadness, and I see his eyes look like mine did in the photograph he took of me.

The realization makes me want to crumble completely, but I manage to hold it together the rest of the day and during his match.

He plays beautifully, of course, and the Greene Falcons officially advance to the next round.

Usually, I hang around after the game, but once the final

whistle blows, I head off to my car with a plan to try out another new coffee shop so I have somewhere to sit and edit my photos.

My routine doesn't change much over the next few weeks—school, homework, gloating parents, Andy's text messages, and free ice cream.

Thankfully, but also not, *The Review* lets me know that since the team has moved so far in the postseason, I'm no longer needed because they officially put their staff sports photographer on the coverage.

Because of that, I talk to Ella about letting Mindy take over for me on behalf of our school paper, saying it's not fair that I've been getting so many front-page photos lately.

Ella doesn't seem to completely buy my excuse, but she goes along with it.

Part of me is devastated to miss out on the sideline view, but logically, I know it's for the best right now.

On the Saturday of the semifinal, I wander around Shadyside with my camera. I've neglected it for weeks, but I desperately need an old friend today, since my actual best friend is in the stands with his boyfriend, cheering Vince on.

I'm just hoping the change of scenery will give me inspiration and help distract me from looking up the score on my phone.

But after a bit of wandering, my stomach rumbles, so I head to a little diner Jake once took me to.

It was right after he got his driver's license, and he had a habit of taking joyrides around the city, burning gas and blasting music.

When we drove past the sign proclaiming "The Second

Best Sandwiches in the City," he thought it was so hilarious that the place absolutely deserved our patronage.

Back then, I was excited to spend time with my brother while sinking my teeth into a sandwich that was wider than my mouth, but now, in my solitude at the window seat, the crunchy sourdough and fresh vegetables don't bring about the same joy.

I brush the crumbs off my fingertips as a flash of golden hair entering the shop catches my attention.

"Abigail?" I blurt out.

"Maren," she returns coolly. "I thought that was you."

I push my plate away as she perches on the stool beside me.

"You never took me up on my offer to show off your portfolio," she says.

"I know."

"Why not?"

I drop my gaze to my hands. "It's just..." I trail off, unsure how to continue.

She sits stoically with her hands on her lap as she waits for me to start speaking again.

I clear my throat. "I wasn't sure if I should."

"I saw you leave that night, remember?" Abigail says. "You brushed right by me, tears in your eyes. I may be a purveyor of art, Maren, but I'm also a human—a *woman,* who has had to make her way in a male-dominated field. I'll be damned if I let another entitled creep take credit for someone else's talent or make them feel uncomfortable in my own gallery."

"Mr. Wilde—"

"Has been barred from ever stepping foot in one of my

galleries," she says firmly. "And although I don't have much pull in academia other than the programs I support, I do have connections that I am happy to put word in with when his contract ends that it should not be renewed."

I blink rapidly. "What?"

"I didn't overhear your conversation, but one of my employees did."

"Oh." I feel heat spread up my cheeks.

"Maren."

Her voice has a sharp edge that calls me to attention before she goes on.

"The art world is a little confusing to some, and even intimidating to most, but let me tell you that it doesn't matter who gives the introduction or who says what about your art. Yes, it helps to know people, to establish connections, but your entire career doesn't thrive or die on whether a second-rate artist currently teaching high school thinks you're pretty."

I gape at her. "But I thought—"

"That I respected him?" She slips off her gloves and unbuttons her coat, officially settling in beside me. "He does occasionally produce decent work, and he knows how much I value fostering the arts for young students around the city, so I've put up with him, but it stops now. Rather, it stopped the minute you were forced to run out of a rather lovely event to escape him."

"Okay," I breathe.

"But with all of his faults, Owen was right about one thing," Abigail says, her tone softening.

"What's that?" I can't help but ask.

"You've got talent."

I chew on my bottom lip. "Thank you."

She laughs. "No need to thank *me*, Maren. I haven't done anything but state the truth. Now, do you have your computer in the bag at your feet so you can show me your portfolio?"

I scramble to pull it out, and then we spend the next hour going through every single piece.

TWENTY-FOUR

The game is well into the second half when I arrive.

As expected with two teams who have made it to the end, it's almost violent how ruthless the style of play is.

I don't bother with the stands, but I don't have that precious pass to get access to the sidelines like I've grown accustomed to. Instead, I walk around the field, positioning myself where I took my favorite game shot, right behind the opponent's goal.

With ten seconds left, Vince is fouled, resulting in a free kick that Uncle Eric waves for him to take.

The other team lines up, creating a defensive wall to try and block out him and the goal.

But I see it.

The little flaw in their lineup.

Without even seeing the statistics or knowing the goalkeeper's preference, I can tell he is going to favor the right side, so I scoot left and hold up my hand, waving for Vince's attention.

His concentration falters slightly as he takes in my presence and reads my signal, but I see understanding register in his eyes almost immediately—see that he trusts so wholly what I see with my eyes, even without being behind a lens.

I drop my hand after the whistle blows, and Vince, with perfect accuracy, kicks the ball, sending it through the gap in coverage to hit the back of the net.

The crowd goes wild at the assumed victory, and his teammates pile on him until the refs blow the whistle, indicating that they need to finish out the clock.

They do, but as soon as the clock runs out, the field is flooded by excited fans, and I get lost in the crowd during the celebration.

I walk around aimlessly, propelled forward by the excitement, but I stop moving the minute I see two people I never thought I'd see at another game.

My parents.

"What are you doing here?" I yell, raising my voice above the crowd's noise.

"We couldn't miss Vince's last game as a Falcon," my mother says, like it's the most obvious thing in the world.

I burst out laughing. "You and Vince are really close these days, huh?"

She blinks. "Well—"

"I just got an internship offer," I cut in. "After school for the spring semester and full-time this summer. A paid internship at a gallery."

My father clears his throat. "I thought we moved past this whole hobby of yours."

"It's not a hobby," I say resolutely.

I feel a large hand land on my shoulder, and I turn to see Uncle Eric beaming with pride.

"That's great news, Maren," he says. "I'm really proud of you, and Jake would be, too."

Those words make my heart pound—not because they hurt but because I know they're true.

"And I'm really proud of *you*," I tell him, bringing him in for a quick hug. "Congratulations, Coach Eric. You deserve it."

"We should celebrate both achievements in a big way next weekend," he suggests.

"Sounds good to me," I admit, then turn to my parents. "You can join us...if you want."

"No," Uncle Eric corrects, patting my back as he glares at them. "You *will* join me and your exceptionally talented daughter, who is about to make money in her field and start off her career *years* ahead of her peers. We *will* be discussing her present and future, and you *will* be just as supportive of her as you were for this game. We're supposed to be the adults here, yet it's Maren who has been stuck navigating around us just because we couldn't get ourselves together or even look at each other after Jake died."

Expressions tight, my parents glance at each other, and the four of us have a silent standoff among the roaring crowd.

"All right," my mother finally says, so quietly I barely register it.

But the agreement is confirmed when my father nods.

"All right," I repeat before we part ways.

I need to get away from them for my own sanity's sake,

and Uncle Eric needs to celebrate with his team.

The bleachers are almost empty at this point, due to the storming of the field, so I make my way over to them, climbing the metal stairs to see the scene from a different view.

Eventually, after what feels like years of shouting and cheers, Uncle Eric drags the players to the locker room, and the massive wave of spectators disperses, heading off to the parking lot to continue their celebrations somewhere else.

I lean against the railing, breathing in the cold November air until it catches in my lungs at the sight of Vince.

He emerges from the visitor locker room, gym bag in tow.

I've studied him enough to know that I'm watching a stride of intention and that when he's chasing down a goal in such a way, he's going to score.

I can't help but sigh happily as he bounds up the stairs toward me, and I have to stop myself from reaching out to him—even though I know I should have done it weeks ago.

"Hey, Vince."

The side of his mouth ticks, withholding a smile.

"Congratulations," I say lightly.

He nods. "Coach Eric tells me you deserve the same sentiment."

"Yes," I say proudly.

"And Andy told me about...the other thing," he adds.

I'm not surprised at my meddling best friend, and part of me is grateful that I don't have to spell it out for Vince myself.

"I'm sorry I didn't tell you," I tell him honestly. "I just

wanted to work it out on my own."

"You don't have to when you have me, Maren," he presses.

I chew on my bottom lip. "I felt like I had to. After going down such a spiral after Jake's death and drowning in my sorrow...I latched onto you, and I guess I didn't want to burden you but also kind of needed to prove to myself that I could get through it."

"How's that working out for you?" Vince asks lightly.

I laugh. "Not totally great, but not bad either."

He reaches for me, and I slide my hand into his easily, not realizing how much I missed his touch until this exact moment.

"And do you feel as though you've proven to yourself what I've known all along?" he presses.

I let out a breath. "I think so."

"Good. Because there's something I want to give you."

Vince bends down to unzip his bag.

"I still have your jersey," I admit.

"This is better than that. I think."

"Well, it kind of seems like I should be giving you something, doesn't it?" I ask with a chuckle.

"Andy told me about your film camera, and it just so happens that, with all my recent free time, my mom and I decided to start unboxing everything in our apartment..."

He stands and offers me a beautiful, vintage Polaroid camera that's far cooler than anything I've ever owned.

"I know there are more modern ones out there that print the pictures right away, but this was my uncle's, and I just, I don't know, thought of you and figured you would like to have it."

I grip it with one hand and wrap the other around the back of his neck. "It's perfect," I assure him. "Thank you."

He slides his hands around my waist. "Can I tell you a secret? It's my last one."

I nod, uncertain my voice will cooperate at this point.

"I have absolutely no idea what I want to do after we graduate," he admits, and it's clearly a relief for him to do so. "Teams have been trying to sign me since I was fifteen years old, and I should have figured this out by now, but I haven't. And oddly enough, I'm okay with that."

Every player strives for perfection.

They want the perfect record, the perfect game, the perfect play.

While Vince is absolutely flawless on the field, untouch-able on so many levels, to me, he's my own personal brand of perfection, so kind, caring, and himself.

And I love that I get this version—the real, uncertain one who isn't afraid to bare it all.

"Well, I've got a final secret to tell you," I say coyly.

"Let's hear it."

I pause. "I'm falling for you, Vince Novak."

He squeezes my waist. "I would have said that, too, but I didn't know it was a secret."

I laugh, and he smiles, revealing his crooked tooth.

And even though this moment between us is surely going to be permanently embedded in my brain, I hold the camera up, angling my arm just so to capture us both, and press the shutter release.

I have a feeling it's going to be one of thousands of happy moments that I document of us together.

Flaws and all.

EPILOGUE

FIVE YEARS LATER

Soccer Star Vince Novak Marries High School Sweetheart

PITTSBURGH — This news is sure to shatter the hearts of Vince Novak's most loyal and hopeful fans, but over the weekend, the U.S. standout center forward tied the knot with long-time girlfriend Maren Montgomery.

Novak, the youngest recorded USMNT player to score a goal in a World Cup, married the award-winning photographer in a small ceremony with immediate family and close friends.

Anderson Crain, a noted fashion magazine editor and frequent collaborator of Montgomery's, presided over the ceremony.

The two met during Novak's final high school season, and tied the knot after dating for more than five years, spanning Novak's one-season college career at Stanford, his two-year stint in the Premier League, then his return to the States, where he was eager to play within MLS.

Montgomery has had an impressive career of her own. Known for her eclectic style of film photography, her works have been featured in several national publications, as well as prestigious galleries. Her first photography book, *Perfect Little Flaws*, is forthcoming this spring.

According to a rep for the newly married couple, the two will honeymoon after Novak's club season concludes.

As always, Lindsay Hallowell, thank you times one million. I'm writing this before you're going to proofread it, but I already know you're going to catch so many of my little stupid mistakes and kill my extra words. I'd be lost without you!

I also need to thank Emily Wright, who keeps me going with her thoughts and cute dog pictures.

And finally, to my family, friends, and all the wonderful people who read my books and support me—it means more to me than you'll ever know.

ACKNOWLEDGMENTS

I have to start by thanking Kilroy, who this book is dedicated to. Not only has she been the most wonderful human in the time I've known her but she's also accepted the role of book photographer, adventure and dance partner, and best friend in stride. I love you!

Christine Wheary, I'm so glad I clicked on that Instagram ad—and that we *finally* got the opportunity to work together. Thank you for your edits and kind words on the early version of this book.

Kelly Lipovich, thank you for creating such a gorgeous and perfect cover! I'm regularly awed by your beautiful work and creative eye—and am lucky to benefit from it.

Jen McDonnell, you're a goddess and a wordsmith, and I'm so grateful to have you and your brain working on my books and generally in my life. Tear me apart, always!

Denise Leora Madre, you're an absolute angel. Your encouragements and nudges have such an impact on my storytelling. Thank you, thank you, thank you.

ABOUT THE AUTHOR

Jennifer Ann Shore is the award-winning and bestselling author of several fiction books, including "Metallic Red," "The Stillness Before the Start," and "The Extended Summer of Anna and Jeremy."

In her decade of working in journalism, marketing, and book publishing, she has gained recognition for her work from companies such as Hearst and SIIA.

Be sure to visit her website (https://www. jenniferannshore.com) and follow her on Twitter (@JenniferAShore), Instagram (@shorely), or your preferred social media channel to stay in touch.